Don't miss the first phenomenal
Inspector Wang Mystery

DEATH OF A BLUE LANTERN
by Christopher West

"The ambivalent morality of modern China is intelligently exposed, but not at the expense of a first-class crime story."
—*The London Times*

"A skillfully contrasted cast of characters . . . totally convincing . . . Everything one can ask for in a crime novel—pace, excitement, and a skillfully convincing portrait of modern China."

—Simon Brett

"Wang is . . . destined to be one of the great fictional detectives, and his gifted creator to be honored as a wry, observant writer of sensitive cultural insight."
—James Melville, *Hampstead and Highgate Express*

"*The Death of a Blue Lantern* does for China what Martin Cruz Smith did for Russia in the Classic *Gorky Park*."
—Oline H. Cogdill, *Florida Sun-Sentinel*

"[A] gripping, ingenious whodunit set in modern China."
—*Buffalo News*

Christopher West's Inspector Wang Mysteries

DEATH OF A BLUE LANTERN
DEATH ON BLACK DRAGON RIVER
DEATH OF A RED MANDARIN

DEATH ON
BLACK DRAGON RIVER

Christopher West

BERKLEY PRIME CRIME, NEW YORK

DEATH ON BLACK DRAGON RIVER

A Berkley Prime Crime Book / published by arrangement with
the author

PRINTING HISTORY
HarperCollins British edition / 1995
Berkley Prime Crime edition / March 1999

All rights reserved.
Copyright © 1995 by Christopher West.
This book may not be reproduced in whole or in part,
by mimeograph or any other means, without permission.
For information address: The Berkley Publishing Group,
a member of Penguin Putnam Inc.,
375 Hudson Street, New York, New York 10014.

The Penguin Putnam Inc. World Wide Web site address is
http://www.penguinputnam.com

ISBN: 0-425-16783-6

Berkley Prime Crime Books are published
by The Berkley Publishing Group,
a member of Penguin Putnam Inc.,
375 Hudson Street, New York, New York 10014.
The name BERKLEY PRIME CRIME and the BERKLEY PRIME CRIME
design are trademarks belonging to Berkley Publishing Corporation.

PRINTED IN THE UNITED STATES OF AMERICA

10 9 8 7 6 5 4 3 2 1

AUTHOR'S NOTE

Many people have helped me, providing inspiration, information, enthusiasm and support. Xiaodi Bell, Jiang Yan, He Yongmei, Mandy Watts, Graham Michelli, the staff at the Great Britain/China Centre and the "Class of 93" at Totleigh Barton. As any writer knows, it's a lonely life at the computer-face; I couldn't have got anywhere without you all; thank you.

I have used the Pinyin system of romanizing Chinese characters, the one currently used in China. It looks fearsome at first sight, but a few rules soon simplify it:

Q	is pronounced	Ch
Zh	is pronounced	J
X	is pronounced	Sh
-ian	is pronounced	-yen

Thus the *Qing* dynasty is pronounced "Ching," *Zhang* "Jang," *Xu* "Shu," *Lian* "Lyen."

Re Chinese names ... The Chinese put their family names first: Wang Anzhuang's brother is Wang Anming, his father was Wang Jingfu. The practice of referring to people by their job titles (e.g. "Teacher Zhang") is common in modern China: the fact that it makes characters in novels much easier for foreigners like us to remember is an added bonus.

NORFOLK, 1998

LIST OF PRINCIPAL CHARACTERS

(family names in capital letters)

WANG Anzhuang	Inspector, Beijing CID
Rosina	His wife
WANG Anming	His brother

Police personnel:

"Wheels" CHAI	Librarian at CID headquarters, Beijing
HUANG	Station Chief, Nanping
KONG	Constable, Nanping

Others (living):

Mr. and Mrs. CHU	Owners of villa
FEI Baoren	Nurse at Nanping Clinic
FEI Zhaoling	Her father
Francine LEI	Partner of Wu Weidong
LIAN Gang	Retired cadre visiting Nanping

MA Kai	Young local criminal
Mrs. MING	Manageress, Nanping Government Guesthouse
PING Li	Research student
WEI	Manager, Nanping Village Industries
WU	Party Secretary, Nanping
WU Weidong	Secretary Wu's son
XIA	Secretary Wu's clerical assistant
YAO (Old Yao)	Secretary Wu's Deputy
ZHANG	Teacher at Nanping Village School

Others (deceased):

SHEN Zirong	Guerilla in Civil War
WANG Jingfu	Father of Wang Anzhuang and Wang Anming. Village Party Secretary 1949–65
XU Yifeng	Daughter of pre-1949 Nanping landlord
ZHANG, the Red Tiger	Local Red Guard Leader in Cultural Revolution

"Political power grows out of the barrel of a gun."

Mao Zedong

PROLOGUE

It was too late to run away, and anyhow, where could they run to? The girl snuggled closer to the old man, pressing herself against his chest and clutching the rough blue denim of his jacket. The young man stood alone, his hands twitching on the handle of a club.

"It's no use," the old man told him. "You'll only make it worse."

The young man spat on the floor. Old Yeye had been a fighter, always standing up for the family honour, but now the oppressors had worn him down. Someone had to be strong; someone had to fight.

But he couldn't bring himself to say this. Silence fell. Then they heard the voices. Still distant, but growing louder every moment: the first group of Red Guards, making their way across the paddy fields to the family home.

"Long live Chairman Mao!"

"Long live the Great Proletarian Cultural Revolution!"

"Death to all Capitalist Roaders!"

Soon the chants were deafening, and coming from all sides. The house was surrounded; the attackers were closing in.

"Come on out and answer for your crimes!" The Red

Guard leader's voice was made doubly inhuman by his use of a megaphone. "You have two minutes. Otherwise we have cans of petrol here and we'll burn you alive."

A great, natural roar went up: "Kill! Kill! Kill!"

The old man shuddered; this wasn't the Chinese way, the gentle, orderly way of Confucius and Meng Zi . . . The girl sobbed. The young man just hated back.

"Ninety seconds!"

"They mean what they say," said Yeye. He looked round the room, at the paintings and the calligraphy that hung there. The family collection, a symbol of all the old man held dear, but now a dangerous liability.

"Take everything off the walls," he ordered.

"You have one minute!"

"You can't think of those things now—" the young man began.

"Do as I say! *We're coming*!" he called out.

"Forty-five seconds!"

"Here." Yeye held out his arms, and the young man loaded him up with scrolls. The girl did the same.

"Thirty seconds!"

The young man wrenched the last pieces off the wall. The character *yong* (eternal) penned in the reign of the Jiaqing Emperor. The boats on the river, forever, or so he had dreamt as a boy, sunlit and tranquil—

"Fifteen! Get those cans ready, Comrades!"

"We're coming!" Yeye called out again. The family ran across their courtyard, bowed down under their burdens as if in anticipation of the humiliations to come. A jeer greeted them as they opened their big oak front door; a crowd of faces stared at them, eyes full of hate.

"Take these," Yeye said to the Red Guard leader, a man known throughout this part of Shandong province as the Red Tiger.

The Red Tiger stepped forward, glanced at what was being offered and sneered. "What are the Four Olds?" he asked.

"Old . . . Some old men?"

"You're ignorant as well as wicked. Old customs, old

habits, old culture, old thinking. What does Chairman Mao want us to do with them?''

"Change them?''

"Destroy them!'' The Red Tiger pushed Yeye away, with such force that the scrolls tumbled out of the old man's arms on to the ground. "Make a pile of these vile things. All of you. We'll have a fire!''

As the order was obeyed, a squat, servile-looking man came up to the leader and whispered in his ear.

"I suppose so,'' came the reply. "It's not for us to question Comrade Kang Sheng. But not too many, mind.''

The man rifled through the scrolls and took a selection, then Guards came and doused the remnants of the collection in petrol.

"Down with the reactionaries!'' shouted someone, who wanted more from the evening than a few paintings going up in smoke.

"Send 'em on a jet-plane ride!'' somebody else added. The Guards' favourite torture involved making people stand bent forward, arms straight behind their backs, for hours on end.

"Put 'em in the cowshed!'' cried a third.

"All in good time, Comrades,'' said the Red Tiger. "We have cultural work to do tonight.'' He took a torch and held it aloft. The crowd fell silent, while the Tiger lowered his torch with slow, almost loving, deliberation. The dry silk and paper ignited at its first touch. For a second it seemed as if the picture scrolls had come to life; they were dancing with the agony of combustion; they were disintegrating into shards of ash and hurling themselves up a tree-high column of flame into the night sky. Then they were nothing. The flames died as quickly as they had arisen. Old Yeye fought back the tears: he must not be seen to react.

"You were wise to hand over these disgusting objects,'' said Red Tiger Zhang. "But don't think all your crimes are forgiven.''

Yeye shook his head humbly: the leader turned away and began to read a long section from *The Thoughts of Chairman Mao*. The mob joined in, the few who didn't know the passage by heart mouthing along, hoping nobody would notice. Yeye sighed with relief; he had saved the lives of his family tonight; he should be grateful. For how long, of course, that was a different matter. But now, in 1967, in China's Cultural Revolution, people like him could only live a day at a time.

1

Inspector Wang Anzhuang of the Beijing Criminal Investigations Department relaxed into his soft-class seat. He put down his paper and returned to staring out at the countryside. Dirt-tracks, wheatfields, long, straight canals lined with poplars: the rural province of Shandong. The province where he'd grown up, the province he still regarded as home, as a bastion of good sense, kindness and continuity in contrast with the crazy, selfish, novelty-obsessed capital where he now worked . . . The train rattled through yet another village. The main street was empty; the inhabitants of Xingnan were enjoying a siesta from the late-summer sun; only the walls were awake, clamouring their bright, hand-painted slogans.

''Use Long March Brand Electric Fans!''

''Good Value, Scientific Design!''

''Hefei No. 2 Electrical Goods Factory Is the Best!''

Then Xingnan was gone. More fields, and a distant pencil line of hills on the horizon. Somewhere up among them was another dozy village, called Nanping . . .

The young woman asleep beside him stirred, turning further into his shoulder. For the ten thousandth time the inspector asked himself if Rosina would really enjoy this trip.

He wanted her to, desperately, and he knew that she wanted to as well. But his new, young wife was Beijing born and bred; many of her friends were artists and intellectuals—how would she find the people among whom Wang had lived the first sixteen years of his life?

"They're not stupid," he told himself. "Not the people my father knew. And anyway, she's not stuck-up, not like some of those friends of hers."

The inspector picked up the paper again, but soon began shaking his head. The news these days . . . More criticism of China from President Clinton. More trouble with Fat Peng, the last imperialist governor of Hong Kong. Anti-Party elements in Chongqing demonstrating against the Three Gorges dam. A hoard of weapons found in a house in Tianjin: guns seemed to be getting everywhere, especially in the wrong hands. But these were urban incidents. For the next three weeks, he and his wife would be away from all this, in the country.

The jeep that picked them up from Jinan station stank of chickens: sacks of fertilizer added a secondary, chemical smell—and took up all the space except for the front seat, onto which the inspector and his wife had had to cram themselves in great discomfort. Then the driver, a lad of about twenty, insisted on driving as if he were at one of those Japanese-style amusement arcades, turning the rural journey into a virtual war with cyclists, donkeys, pedestrians and fellow maniacs at the wheels of trucks. Only once they had passed through the town of Wentai and entered the hills did things calm down. There was little traffic, and the lad had to get his kicks by throwing the vehicle round each bend. Wang tried protesting, but the driver said he had a schedule to keep to.

"This road was just a track last time I came here," the inspector said wistfully.

"That's Secretary Wu's doing," the young man replied. 'He got it tarmacked—well, it must be five years ago."

Wang felt a stab of guilt. Was it really that long since he'd been here?

They lurched round another corner, and a gaunt brick needle came into view on the skyline. "Ah!" said Wang. 'The hundred-Buddha pagoda!"

"The no Buddha pagoda, we call it nowadays," the driver replied.

Another stab of guilt, this time for the inspector's generation rather than anything personal. In 1967, the hundred or so Buddhas that had stared out from the old brick tower for centuries had been smashed to pieces. At forty-two, Wang was just the right age to have been involved.

"It could have been a real tourist attraction," the driver went on. "People from the cities would have come to see it. Overseas Chinese, too. Maybe even big-noses. Big nose, big wallet! But of course those stupid bloody Red Guards . . ." A look of embarrassment suddenly crossed the driver's face. "You weren't . . . ?"

Wang smiled. "No, I was in the Army: the one place where you didn't have to do that sort of thing."

The young man looked relieved. "I thought so. You got a medal, didn't you? Then you became a gold-badge. Solving murders and so on. Assistant Xia told me all about you."

The jeep rounded another corner. Ahead of them was a valley, flat and fertile at the bottom, with hills rising up all round it. At the far end lay Nanping village.

Home.

"You'll notice a lot of changes," said the driver as they passed the first houses.

"Well . . ." The outer village was exactly the same jumble of pathways, small fields and old brick-walled homesteads it had always been.

"Look ahead. And up a bit."

"Ah." The hillside straight ahead of them had sprouted clutches of villas: square, flat-roofed, double-storeyed, garishly painted. And expensive.

"Progress," said the young man. "I'm going to have one of those places by the time I'm twenty-five."

"How?"

"Hard work!"

They passed the old bell tower and entered the main street. The buildings all seemed to have grown a storey or two, and the roadway was busy with bikes, trucks, wooden handcarts and three-wheeled "iron cow" tractors. Pedestrians, a few in the old Mao suit but most sporting bright T-shirts or fancy, embroidered blouses, dodged these vehicles, either to cross the road or because the pavement was filled by market stalls and piles of produce. Nanping was clearly prospering. Wang turned to his wife with a grin. She stared wanly back—didn't she like this scene? The inspector frowned, then looked back at the street. The noise! The life! Only down the alleyways off to the left was there anything to depress—glimpses of the poor quarter of Nanping, the "old village." From what he could see, nothing much had improved there. Which meant that his brother—

"I'm seven minutes late," the driver said suddenly. "All right if I make a delivery then take you to the guesthouse?"

Wang reached for the letter from the local Party Secretary promising "special transport" from Jinan station. Then he nodded his head. He'd worked hard accumulating extra leave; he wanted to make this visit relaxing and trouble-free.

They carried on up the main street, past Yang's Boarding House and the walled compounds of Police and Party HQ, to North Square, a paved area at the top of the village. The ramshackle tin-roofed factory on the far northern side had been Wentai Brigade No. 9 Agricultural Implements Plant in Wang's youth: a banner now announced it as Nanping Village Industries Corporation.

The driver stopped by its gate and got out. "Won't be long."

Silence fell. Wang turned to his wife and said: "Welcome to Nanping!" She opened the door, half climbed, half collapsed out of it and was sick.

North Square boasted a fountain that never worked, two cypress trees and an old millstone on which Wang had ground corn by hand as a teenage boy. The millstone was now a seat, and Wang led Rosina towards it.

"I'm fine," she said blearily.

"Sit down and rest. I'll tell that damned driver to take the cases up to the guesthouse, and we can get a taxi later." Wang had no idea if there were any taxis in Nanping, but he'd find a vehicle somehow.

"I'll walk. When I'm feeling a bit better. You know I like to walk . . ."

Wang nodded: that was one of the reasons they had come here.

An old man was sitting on the stone, smoking a pipe. Wang thought he recognized him, and tried to remember the fellow's name. Then the man looked up. Mao, that was it. Pigtail Mao. The name came from—

"*Ai!*" The old man had leapt to his feet. He was staring at the visitors with a look of undisguised horror. The inspector opened his mouth to speak, but the old fellow had already turned his back and was hobbling away as fast as he could.

Wang tried calling, but this only seemed to make the man hobble quicker. So he gave a shrug and helped his wife the last few steps to the stone. Rosina sank on to it and hid her head in her hands; her body began heaving as if she were crying. He sat down beside her, put an arm round her shoulder and whispered reassurances in her ear.

"I know this has been a bad start . . ." he said.

Rosina lowered her hands and turned to him. "That old man's face!" she said, then resumed her helpless laughter.

The Government Guesthouse was halfway up the hillside, a location it now shared with the homes of the newly rich. The inspector and his wife, who had walked up to it, were greeted on the front steps by the manageress, Mrs. Ming, who showed them to their room. They didn't have to present any ID or sign any book: Mrs. Ming was happy with the letter from Secretary Wu.

"I said we'd be well looked after," said Wang, as they took stock of their accommodation, a spacious bedsit with a bathroom en suite and heavy old-fashioned furniture: a silk-covered bed, two chairs, a writing desk by the window, a massive wardrobe and chest of drawers.

"I want you to make friends here," Wang went on. "Not just people I knew, but new people. You must feel free to do that."

"I shall," said Rosina. "But I shall make a special effort with your brother—the only Wang left in Nanping. Don't try and stop me."

Wang didn't look as pleased as he perhaps should have been at this promise. "Anming can be very difficult sometimes."

"I spend my life with difficult people. Now let's get unpacked. Let's make ourselves at home."

They walked up a path that led from the back of the guesthouse to a pass at the top of the valley: they sat on a rock and looked down over Nanping—concrete and straight lines in the newer parts; tiles and bricks and corrugated iron in the twisting alleys of the "old village"; the chequerboard fields and the outlying homesteads; around them all, the hills like protecting arms, rocky and jagged outcrops in some places, gentle terraces in others.

"It's beautiful," said Rosina. "And so green. I was expecting something much starker."

"We're lucky," Wang replied, dropping into the proprietorial "we" as if he'd never left the place. "We've got some fine springs up here." He smiled. "Anming and I used to play in them—racing toy boats, swimming in the pools. And frog-hunting, of course. If we caught one, we'd take it home for our little sister."

Rosina smiled at the thought.

"Then we'd have frog for supper," Wang went on. "Delicious!"

Rosina grimaced and pointed into the valley on the other side of the pass, a steeper, narrower feature than the generous horseshoe around Nanping. "What's down there?" she asked.

"That's Snake Valley. There are some more fields just round the corner, and a track leads on to Weipowan, the

next village. There's a Revolutionary memorial, too. It's a
nice walk—if I can remember the way. Fancy a try?''

Rosina glanced at her watch and nodded.

"There was a gun battle back in 'forty-seven," said
Wang as they began descending the new path. "An ambush: the Guomindang troops were waiting in those trees;
a lot of partisans were killed. They put up the memorial in
the early fifties, and Father used to take us there every year
on the anniversary. He'd give us a lecture on duty, patri-
otism and so on. It was very moving. He meant it—not like
so many of the speeches you hear nowadays."

Rosina, who tried to avoid speeches wherever possible,
shook her head.

"Dear Father—I can see him now!" Wang went on. "At
his desk in Party HQ, surrounded by paper. Getting home
just in time to tuck us into bed. The light from his lamp
burning all hours of the night—with the wick on low because he didn't want to waste paraffin, which belonged to
the People. Mother never complained. They were doing
their duty, you see, to China, to the Party. Not like modern
cadres."

"No . . . There are other reasons to live, Anzhuang."

Wang pondered the comment for a while, then said:
"Maybe . . . It certainly killed him. He'd sometimes go
days without rest. During the Land Reform Movement he
didn't sleep for a week."

Rosina nodded. History had never been her strong subject, but she knew that soon after Liberation, the Party had
ordered that everybody in the countryside be classified as
landlord, rich-peasant, middle-peasant or poor-peasant category, so that land could be reallocated. As village Party
Secretary, Wang's father would have been in charge of this
process.

"Most cadres made their decisions in minutes," Wang
went on. "Father made files on everyone and spent hours
worrying about them. He knew what would happen, you
see. He was a real Communist: he cared about people."

Rosina felt a shiver of disapproval at these sentiments,
but suppressed it. "What *did* happen?" she asked instead.

"A mob tried to lynch the landlords and rich peasants. Father said it was him and two very scared militiamen against about a hundred angry farm-workers armed with clubs and pitchforks and whatever else they could get their hands on."

"And?"

"Father talked them round, of course. He told them that everyone in New China should have the chance to reform—even the biggest landlords, the Xus. People respected him so much, they backed off." Wang smiled at the memory, then looked glum again. "Not that it did any good in the long run."

"Oh. How so?"

"During the Cultural Revolution, Old Xu was clubbed to death, and so was his son. The daughter . . ." He paused. "*Aiya*, you don't want to hear this. It's getting cold. Let's head for home."

The new arrivals ate alone in the guesthouse's small, functional dining room.

"There's only one other person staying," Mrs. Ming explained, "and he prefers to eat in his rooms."

Rosina, gregarious by nature, was puzzled. "How unfriendly," she said.

"He's very distinguished," Mrs. Ming replied. "A retired cadre. I'm sure he's earned his peace."

"What's he doing here?"

"I don't know. On holiday, I'd imagine."

"Here?" Rosina said quickly, then looked embarrassed. "I didn't mean—"

Wang laughed, but Mrs. Ming looked offended. "We have distinguished people visiting here. Most have some past link with the place, but not all: they come because they find our village tranquil. In the old days, officials used to retire to private gardens and so on. I don't see why people who have spent their lives in the service of the New China shouldn't have a similar privilege."

"No . . ." said Wang, chastened. "We shall have to go round and introduce ourselves to him sometime." He took

a piece of the five-flower pork Mrs. Ming had just brought
in, dipped it in vinegar and ate. "Meanwhile, I'm going to
eat. Proper Shandong food!"

"You seemed really sad up there on the pass," said Rosina, once Mrs. Ming had gone. "If there's anything you
want to talk about . . ."

"No," Wang replied. Rosina would talk anything out:
the new, Western way of doing things. Wang was used to
the old, Chinese way: keep quiet, keep face. "There's more
to this revisiting business than I imagined. Silly of me not
to have realized." He took his wife's hand and picked up
a glass. "We're going to enjoy ourselves here. There's the
dinner tomorrow night; the weather looks set fair; there's
people to meet, which you always enjoy. If a few unwel-
come memories come back, I'll deal with them. *Mei
wenti!*" No problem!

"No problem," Rosina echoed, and raised her glass.

2

The red metal star over the gates of Party HQ glinted in the sun.

"New coat of paint," said Wang approvingly.

"In our honour?" Rosina replied.

A policeman at the gate asked for their papers: Wang showed them and the couple walked across an uneven courtyard to the main offices, a two-storey concrete building with damp stains down the side and small, shuttered windows.

The Party. Rosina kept it from her artier friends, but she was a member, just like her husband. Not out of conviction, not now, but because it helped at work. Sometimes she felt this was wrong—but plenty of other people did the same. She spied on colleagues as seldom as possible; when forced to do so, she would report purely professional details, much to the annoyance of her superiors. She often enjoyed the fantasy that one morning she'd wake up and all politicians, Party officials and so on had vanished, leaving people to get on with their own lives. But she knew this was just a fantasy, and that if she wanted to remain ward sister at one of the capital's top hospitals, she had to be in the Party.

They reached the main block. A receptionist behind a

grille asked to see their papers again, then phoned through to someone.

"Secretary Wu's assistant will be down in a moment," said the receptionist. "In the meantime, if you'd like to go in and take a seat . . ."

Wang and Rosina sat on a hard wooden bench in the front hall and glanced through some agricultural magazines, until a door opened and a young man in a bright-yellow shirt and fashionably tight trousers emerged.

"My name's Xia," he said, holding out a hand. "I'm Secretary Wu's clerical assistant. He's out at the moment. He asked me to show you around."

The young man led them through the door into a small room with a high, closed window and a striplight. "This is my office." His desk was tidy: papers in the middle, a fan to one side and a photograph of a young woman on the other.

"Your wife?" Rosina asked him, pointing at the picture.

"Girlfriend," Xia said with cheeky pride, then opened the next door into the Party Secretary's office. Secretary Wu worked in a room about eight times the size of his assistant's. There were filing cabinets all round the walls: his desk stood in the centre, as lonely as a desert island. On it, papers were piled high in two trays.

"Some things haven't changed," said Wang. "All that bureaucracy! Mind if I go in?"

"Er, no. Of course not."

Wang crossed to the desk and sat in the Secretary's chair. He tried not to look at the papers in front of him, but like all good detectives he was curious.

Re: Local "environmental" protestors . . .

Aiya, did they have that sort of thing out here, too?

"We have a fine banqueting room upstairs," said Assistant Xia.

Wang turned over the corner of the top paper. "Surveillance is being maintained at a discreet—"

"It was redecorated recently. You should see it, Inspector."

Wang took the hint. They made their way up an uncarpeted staircase, past a spittoon and a dying pot-plant, to a room with a purple carpet and horrible lime-green wallpaper.

"Secretary Wu's entertaining you here this evening, isn't he?" said Xia.

"Yes. You're not invited?"

The young assistant blushed. "I'm too junior. But all the top people in the village will be there. And your brother, of course."

"Of course," said Wang without enthusiasm. Stay off the booze, Anming, for all our sakes.

"Ganbei!" Cheers! Party Secretary Wu raised a glass of powerful, clear *Maotai* spirit. "To the memory of Wang Jingfu!"

The inspector smiled at the sound of his father's name.

"Ganbei!"

A white-coated waiter brought in yet another main course, Yellow River carp with sweet and sour sauce, and placed it on the carousel. Wang, as guest of honour, took the first portion. Then Secretary Wu, as host . . . Wang watched as the fish made its way round the table. The elderly, Mao-suited Deputy Secretary Yao and his elderly, Mao-suited wife took identical small portions. The local police chief, a burly man in his fifties, spooned himself a big chunk. The manager of Nanping Village Industries, Wei, took a similar amount but with infinitely more finesse. Top people . . . Then Wang's brother Anming reached out two shaking chopsticks and managed both to secure two segments of meat and to transfer them to his bowl—a feat which made his red face glow even brighter.

Secretary Wu commenced a formal speech of welcome.

"Wang Jingfu, our Secretary from Liberation till his tragic death in 1965, was admired and respected by everyone in Nanping. That death deprived us of a leader of real quality . . ."

Secretary Wu was nearly six feet tall. His strong voice belonged to someone used to giving orders; his stiff posture to a man who did not like having those orders questioned.

"Ten years of turmoil and disorder followed his demise," he went on (alluding, of course, to the Cultural Revolution). 'And only when the Party issued its call to follow the Four Modernizations was government truly restored the way Wang Jingfu would have wanted. On instructions from both national, provincial and county leadership, Nanping plunged into the sea of commerce. The success of this brave act is now, fifteen years on, visible everywhere. Only recently, our village was singled out in the provincial press as a model of economic reform and openness. Our factory produces tools, clothing and machine parts that are sold all over the province. This fine fish apart, all the food that has graced our table this evening has come from local cooperative enterprises." Wu paused. "Now, I know that in the community at large, voices are beginning to criticize this progress, saying 'enough and no further.' Wang Jingfu would not have been a part of this reactionary chorus."

Deputy Yao and his wife nodded in unison. The police chief made a grunt of approval. Wang's brother Anming and the young factory manager both did nothing.

Dissent?

Secretary Wu's seemingly permanent smile broke for an instant—then he continued his speech with practised ease. "Wang Jingfu joined the Party in 1938 . . ."

A life of Wang's father followed, then compliments to the two guests, then a toast. "To our visitors! *Ganbei!*" Wu drained his tumbler of *Maotai* then sat down. Deputy Yao took the floor.

"Long live the Party! Long live the People! That was the motto of Wang Jingfu, a man whose life bears comparison with that of the Good Soldier Lei Feng."

Wang groaned inwardly at the mention of this semi-mythical worthy. This was going to be one of *those* speeches . . . The secret was to fix a smile on your face and nod occasionally. And not, as the inspector had seen other, less practised listeners do, to fall asleep. (Or if you did doze off, don't snore.)

"Wang Jingfu always supported the Four Cardinal Principles. He accepted the paramountcy of Marxism, Leninism and Mao Zedong Thought; he believed in Socialism, and trusted the Party and the democratic dictatorship of the People. He never ceased to struggle against imperialism, liberalism, ultra-leftism, rightist deviationism, Soviet-style revisionism . . .''

Wang found himself looking round the table again. He must have known all these people, but had little recollection of them. Deputy Yao, he remembered, had always been unimaginative and hard-working; Secretary Wu ambitious. During the Cultural Revolution Yao had been criticized by Red Guards and simply gone back to working in the fields. Wu had survived the madness by playing along with it. Of the man who had run Nanping in those days, Red Tiger Zhang, there was no trace or mention . . .

Deputy Yao was holding up a glass. ''To the Communist Party of China! May it last ten thousand years! *Ganbei!*''

''*Ganbei!*'' Wang replied, perfectly on cue.

The old man sat down and his wife stood up. Her voice was high, sharp and, like Secretary Wu's, used to giving orders: as head of the Nanping Women's Association she would have plenty of opportunity for doing that. In her speech she praised Wang's late mother for her resilience during difficult times (glancing, as she said this, at Anming), then described her own efforts to enforce the one-child policy, particularly via strict adherence to marriage quotas. She still tried to prevent marriage between classes, she said: such prevention might no longer be fashionable in big cities, but in Nanping she made sure it was still hard for the offspring of old exploiters to pollute pure working-class stock. Mrs. Yao concluded with a criticism of foreign notions of romantic love, which ''eat into the political fabric of society.'' ''The example set by Party members on this issue is of the utmost importance,'' she added, with a steely glance at Rosina.

Her husband gave her particularly loud applause when she sat down.

Then it was the turn of the police chief, whose name was Huang. He got nervously to his feet, brushed some dandruff off the lapels of his nylon suit, proposed a toast to justice, then delivered a short account of local public-security matters. Wang listened with interest, even though he had promised Rosina—and himself—that he would have as little to do with the police as possible.

"A number of thefts have occurred in the area," said the police chief. "We are making excellent progress in their solution—but if the inspector would care to give us the benefit of his expertise, we would be extremely grateful."

Wang thought of his promise, then nodded his head: this was a matter of politeness. Rosina shot him a heavy glance.

Wei, the well-groomed boss of Nanping Village Industries, spoke next. His speech, also brief, was full of economic terms that Wang didn't understand—except for a short homily on the importance of decisiveness in all kinds of leadership.

Quite right, Wang said to himself, then happened to glance at Secretary Wu, who was glaring at the speaker with unconcealed hostility. Wang looked away, embarrassed; when he looked back, Wu's politician's smile had reappeared.

"To prosperity!" said Wei.

"To prosperity!"

Then it was Anming's turn to speak.

Wang's brother got slowly to his feet, then began fiddling in the pockets of his jacket. The polite silence that welcomes a new speaker grew longer and longer and ever more strained.

Secretary Wu broke it. "It's getting late. We don't *all* have to make speeches!"

"No," Anming replied. "I have something prepared. Somewhere. I just seem to have, er, mislaid it." He searched a bit more, then shook his head. "I'll do without it. As head of the family, I'd like to say that younger brother Anzhuang is most welcome to return to his old home after—how long is it? Especially as he comes with a lovely wife. My brother has always had excellent taste in women!" He gave a crude laugh; Wu gave a scowl of disapproval; Anming began rifling through his pockets again, finally pulling out a sheet of paper which he then dropped on the floor. "Fuck!" he exclaimed. More silence. Then: "A good speech is a short speech!" He picked up a glass. "To beauty, a toast! *Ganbei!*"

"To beauty," everyone round the table echoed. "*Ganbei!*"

"Now, Lin Xiangyu . . ." said Secretary Wu, using Rosina's official, Chinese name.

Rosina shook her head. "My husband will speak for both of us."

Mrs. Yao frowned at her. Rosina understood why, but she disliked making speeches as much as she disliked listening to them: she either bored herself stupid, or was amusing but said things she regretted later. Wang, on the other hand, enjoyed it. So let him get on with it.

The inspector warmed to his task at once, making general observations about the high quality of leadership and deputy leadership available to the village, echoing the importance of the one-child policy to the Four Modernizations, restating how much he was looking forward to visiting the local police station, praising Nanping Village Industries Corporation for its contribution to the area's evident prosperity, thanking his elder brother for his sincere welcome, then proposing a toast to everyone present.

"*Ganbei!*"

"*Ganbei!*"

The moment the last draughts of *Maotai* were drained, the scraping of chairs announced that the banquet was over. For most of the participants there was work to do early next morning.

"My driver will take you back to your hotel," said Secretary Wu. "I'm sorry we are unable to provide a car full time."

Wang smiled. "I wouldn't want one. My wife and I are both keen walkers."

They left the dining room for the sharp, evening air of the compound, where a VW Shanghai was waiting.

"If there is anything you need, contact me," said Wu. 'There is a telephone at the hotel. My work number is listed; my home number is eight-three-two."

With that, he turned away. Wang and Rosina got into the car. As they drove out of the front entrance, Wang saw his brother Anming take a rusty lampless bicycle out of a rack, mount it and wobble out into the road.

"Is it curable?" he asked Rosina, who had recently taken a course in contemporary Western psychology.

"Only if he wants to be cured."

So much for contemporary Western psychology. "Nobody could want to be like that!"

"Everybody has dark moments. You weren't too happy when I first met you."

"No . . ." He had met Rosina at the most difficult part of his "Blue Lantern" investigation, at a time when he had felt his whole world falling apart. "I sorted myself out, though. Anming doesn't want to, and that's his problem."

The car reached North Square: the tarmac ended here, and the vehicle began to bump up the ever-steepening hill.

"This visit to the police station . . ." said Rosina.

"Formality. Politeness. I promise."

She looked into his eyes, then nodded. He meant it.

The road got bumpier. They were up among the new villas now. They passed one, its lights blazing to advertise that the owner could afford to waste electricity. Wang thought of his father working by minimal illumination, and then about Secretary Wu: if the local boss had a private telephone number, that meant he no longer lived in the old flat in the Party compound but probably owned one of these flashy places, too.

Progress?

The car put them down by the gate of the guesthouse, and the visitors from the big city walked arm-in-arm up the path. They entered their suite; Rosina went straight over to the bed and stretched out on it. Wang fetched glasses of water from the bathroom. All that *Maotai* . . .

"Thanks," said Rosina, draining hers in one. She looked at her husband. "You must have been proud with all the things they said about your parents."

"I was. Of course. I'd like to have heard more about modern Nanping though."

"They're still too busy arguing about it."

Wang laughed: Confucius had been wrong about intelligent women. "I guess we'll find out what that was all about in time."

"I'm sure we will. Right now . . ." Rosina patted the space beside her; the inspector lay down; they kissed; Wang ran his hand down her back to her buttocks; the official world of banquets, duty and rules seemed suddenly absurd and unreal.

3

The crowing of a rooster awoke Rosina at half past five.

"My head . . ." she moaned.

Wang, who wasn't feeling too hot either, grunted in sympathy.

Another crow.

"That bloody chicken," Rosina went on. "I'd like to wring its neck."

"I'll ask Mrs. Ming if we can have it for dinner tonight," said Wang.

Rosina didn't smile, but then she wouldn't have done if he had told the funniest joke in the world.

Soon after, noise came thundering through from the adjoining rooms: an old-fashioned bell alarm clock; the sound of someone and their pet elephant shuffling about; a door slamming. Then came peace. Rosina had just drifted back to sleep when their own bedside telephone rang. Wang fumbled for it, dragging the receiver off its cradle to his ear.

"Inspector Wang? Station Chief Huang here. You expressed an interest in visiting our HQ."

"Yes, er . . ."

"I haven't got you out of bed, have I?"

"No. Of course not. Been up for ages."

"Good." There was a silence. "Would this morning be suitable?"

"Er . . ."

"This afternoon? Four o'clock?"

"Fine."

"Who the hell was that?" Rosina hissed as Wang replaced the phone.

"That policeman."

"Ah. Remember your promise."

"I will."

The rooster let out another crow, its loudest and most braggart yet. Rosina moaned and hid her head in the pillow.

Wang walked down into Nanping alone. He turned off the main street into the "old village," wandering down the narrow, half-paved alleys between the grey-brick courtyard walls and the old-style houses with their overhanging eaves and big wooden latticework doors. His nose puckered at the smell of rotting vegetation, woodsmoke and drains; the children in tatty cast-off clothes saddened him, though they seemed happy enough. More than anything else, he felt shame at his brother, who lived here—not out of some idealistic commitment to sharing the life of the poor, but because he couldn't afford anywhere better.

Wang wondered if he'd remember the way to Tinker's Alley. He didn't. After passing the same noodle house twice, he went in and asked. A morose teenager cleaning tables to a rock tape grudgingly gave him instructions. Incorrect ones, but they led him to a spot Wang did recall, from which . . .

Courtyard Four had a blackened oak door. Wang knocked, and an old woman answered.

"Wang Anming? Who wants to see him?"

"His brother."

"Oh. You'd better come in."

Anming lived on one side of a courtyard which would have belonged to one family years ago, but which was now divided between three. The quad would have then been full

of beautiful flowers or practical vegetables, but was now
littered with odd bits of rubbish. Would anyone really need
a broken bedstead, a tea-chest with a hole in it, a rusty iron
or an eviscerated Panda black-and-white TV again?

"That's his place over there," the woman went on,
pointing at the shabbiest-looking rooms. "But he'll be at
work now: I heard him get up for the early shift."

Wang smiled in admiration of his brother's constitution,
then reminded himself that seasoned drinkers seem to have
incredible powers of recovery. In the short term. He crossed
to his brother's window and looked in through the dusty
pane. A mess, just as he'd expected.

"So you've come all the way from Beijing?" said the
woman.

"Yes."

"Families should be like that."

Wang grinned with guilty embarrassment.

"He's a good neighbour," the woman went on, "except
when he's, er, ill. He'll do anything to help out—if you
ask him, that is: he keeps himself to himself otherwise.
Well, you know him already—"

"I ought to know him better. Tell me, does he always
drink too much, or is it just in bouts?"

She showed no surprise at his directness. "Bouts. He'll
stay off the stuff for weeks, then suddenly he's back on it
again. It's a terrible thing, Mr. Wang."

"I know. Any idea what sets him off?"

"My husband reckons it's something to do with the
moon. I say it's just different things each time. Problems:
we all have them."

"And he's in a drinking phase now?"

"I'm afraid so. A bad one—it's been several months
now."

Wang's spirits sank. "Any idea why?"

"No." But she glanced away as she said this, which
meant she was probably lying.

"You have no idea at all?"

"No. Well, yes. Seeing as you're family . . . It was that
girl."

"Girl?"

"Young woman: when you get to my age everyone under about thirty looks like a child! She came to visit him here. Quite often. And then she stopped. I think they had a row."

"So this was a love affair?"

"I don't know. All I know is that when she stopped visiting, he started drinking. And he hasn't stopped, so it must have been serious. Poor Mr. Wang." There was genuine sympathy in her voice: Anming was lucky to have such a neighbour.

"And you've no idea who this visitor was?"

"No." This looked to be a truthful reply.

"Describe her for me. Height. Build. Clothing." The inspector reminded himself he wasn't on duty. "It might help me to help him."

"Ordinary height. Build? Slim. Healthy-looking. Attractive," the neighbour added with a note of envy. "Western-style clothes. A city girl, I'd imagine." She paused. "Your brother has a right to run his own life—but we're fond of him, and we don't like to see him in a bad way. Maybe he'd listen to you. Tell him to find someone his own age: a nice widowed lady or someone who missed out first time around—with these marriage quotas there are some good women going to waste . . ."

"I don't think he'd listen to me," Wang replied sadly. "Did the visitor ever speak to anyone here?"

"Not to me. I don't know about anyone else. She seemed suspicious of us, but I guess if you were having a love affair with a much older man, you would be."

"Yes." That aspect of Nanping hadn't changed. Wang pondered some other questions to ask, but decided they would be too intrusive.

"Can I offer you some tea?" said the woman. Traditional Shandong hospitality: he accepted with pleasure.

The inspector walked slowly back through the smelly alleyways of Nanping's old village. Various thoughts ran through his head. Poor Anming. Then: bugger "poor Anm-

ing!'' It was typical of his brother to find a woman way
out of his reach, someone who was a whole lot of things
he wanted to be but wasn't. The rest of mankind has to
settle for what they are . . . Then Wang reflected that he,
Anzhuang, had never settled for what he was. He'd always
wanted to be the best. But he'd always gone about self-
improvement practically, step by step. And it had worked.
Maybe it was time to give a little back. But how could he,
to Anming, in practice? This visit apart, he had no time.
He'd like more time—but he had too much work. Anming
had never worked at anything. And now look at him. Serve
him right!

Rosina, revived by a mysterious concoction Mrs. Ming had
prepared, was eager to walk and get lots of fresh air. Wang,
for different reasons, felt the same. They went up to the
pass again and stood looking down at the winding track
they had taken last night into Snake Valley.

"You don't have to go there again if you don't want,"
said Rosina.

"That's silly," Wang replied with studied determination.
"The odd bad memory is bound to come back. I can take
it."

They set off. It had become a lovely day: a lark sang in
the sky and one of the numerous irrigation channels chat-
tered back a reply.

"It was cold-blooded murder!" Wang exclaimed suddenly.

"What was?"

"What happened to Old Xu and his son. And his daughter, Yifeng—well, they didn't actually kill her, just sent her
away to a labour camp in Heilongjiang to freeze to death."

The sun went behind a cloud. Heilongjiang—Black
Dragon River—is China's northernmost province, with
nothing between it and the Arctic except Siberia.

"This was during the Cultural Revolution?" Rosina
asked.

"That's right. 1967. I was away. I got a letter about it
from Anchun. She was shocked: someone had just taken

the two men out of their cowshed and bashed their heads in with iron bars.''

Rosina winced.

''They even accused Xu Yifeng of it, at first,'' Wang went on. ''I mean, have you ever heard of anything so ridiculous? She was a slight, gentle creature. Artistic. She could no more have killed them than she could have throttled a tiger.'' He shook his head. ''The more I think about it, the more angry I feel.''

''It was a long time ago.''

''Yes. But it was still a vile accusation. They were evil, those people.''

Rosina nodded. ''Was Xu Yifeng beautiful?''

''Yes. Very.''

''And you were in love with her?''

''No!'' Wang looked shocked. ''Well, not really. I found her attractive, of course—plenty of guys did. But I was more in love with the Army than Xu Yifeng.'' He sighed. 'I suppose you think I ought to have done something to help her. But I couldn't. I was away: when I came back on my first leave, she'd gone . . . Hell, even if I had been around, there'd have been nothing I could have done. You don't remember those days. The old Party Secretary in Weipowan had been paraded through the streets in a dunce's cap a few weeks before: Father had made enough enemies to make us a prime target, too. Coming to the defence of Xu Yifeng would have got us all locked up, maybe even killed: Mother, Anchun, me—even the good Red Guard Anming.''

The inspector scowled then began walking again.

''Your brother was a Red Guard?'' Rosina asked.

''Oh yes, a proper little Mao worshipper. He's always been weak.'' Wang's pace quickened, as if he were eager to escape this place again.

''Here it is,'' said Wang suddenly. ''The path to that memorial. I'd like to go and see it.''

''OK,'' said Rosina.

They made their way up the slope to a circle of pine

trees, in the middle of which was a square of concrete, now cracked and sprouting grass. At one end was a stone bench, at the other a small obelisk topped by a five-pointed star with traces of red paint on it. Rosina could still read the inscription down the front of the obelisk. *Revolutionary heroes will never perish.* Then there was a list of names on the plinth, and a note—"Killed in Ambush, July 23rd 1947." She knew the patriotic sadness she should feel in such places, but somehow rarely felt in the mood nowadays. The world had moved on.

"Why have they let it get into such a state?" Wang muttered. He bent down, and began wrenching grass out of the cracks. "I mean, look at those bloody weeds over there!"

Rosina did so. "They're figwort," she said.

"What?"

She picked a stem up and examined it. "Zhejiang figwort. A medicinal plant. It grows a lot in the south, but must be pretty rare this far north. It has a wide range of uses: I wonder if the local medics know about it?"

"Perhaps you'd better tell them. If I'm going to be visiting the local police station, you might as well see the village clinic. It's down the end of the main street, near the bell tower."

Rosina pulled up a piece of the plant and examined its root. "I'll do that," she said with sudden determination.

"Inspector!" Station Chief Huang shook Wang vigorously by the hand and led him into his office. "Constable Kong, get our visitor some tea!"

A young man writing a report in very slow, deliberate characters stood up and left the room. Wang sat down on an old wooden chair and looked round him.

"I expect this is all rather primitive compared to Qianmen East Street," the chief went on.

"I wouldn't say that."

The chief looked disappointed. "But you all have computers on your desks, don't you?"

"No."

"And videolinks?"

"No. I have a telephone. It's black and made of Bakelite, exactly like this one."

"Oh. But there's a central mainframe? For records, fingerprints, blood types and so on?"

"Yes. An expert can get a lot of information out of their computer terminal. The rest of us have to be nice to the experts." Wang smiled and pointed out of the window. "Your motorbikes are newer than ours."

"They're Chinese. I bet you have Japanese ones."

The constable returned with two mugs of tea.

"Here's one area where we can match you Beijing boys," said the chief, handing over a mug with a proud smile. 'This stuff is grown and processed locally."

Wang took a sip.

"Like it?" the chief asked.

It was revolting. "Delicious!" Wang lied. "Now tell me about these robberies."

The chief crossed to a map of the area with pins in. "There have been four thefts in the last couple of months. All from villas on the hillside. Entry is by various means—a window forced open, a door-lock picked. They know when the houses are going to be unoccupied. And because those villas are so far apart and have walled private gardens, the bastards can take their time. No one's watching or listening."

"Found any prints?"

"Not so far."

"Tool marks?"

"No."

"They must have left some traces: soil from shoes, animal or human hairs."

"The soil is all local. Hairs . . ." The local policeman grinned with embarrassment. "We don't really have the means to analyse that sort of evidence. I suppose in Beijing, you just do a quick DNA test, check the result on computer—"

"And send a robot out to make the arrest. That's right. You've got files on the crimes, of course?"

"Of course."

"May I see?"

The burglars had stolen the usual stuff: videos, cameras, money, jewellery and, in one case, a piece of calligraphy. There were photographs of some of the missing items: presumably the owner had thought this was a precaution against theft.

"That's nice," said Wang, holding up the photo of the calligraphy.

The chief grunted.

"It looks old," Wang went on. "Does anyone know how much it was worth?"

Another grunt.

Wang looked at the calligraphy more closely. He would love to collect traditional Chinese art, but such hobbies were beyond the pocket of an honest policeman. But he was not jealous of those who could afford it: in modern China plenty of people had money and wasted it; he admired anyone who spent what they had on decent things.

"I'd like to meet the owner," he said.

The local policeman looked surprised. "I think it was taken as an afterthought. Stuff like that is hard to sell round here. It's the electrical goods that shift."

"Maybe," Wang replied with an enigmatic smile. Station Chief Huang stared at him for a moment, then gave another grunt. If that was what the inspector wanted . . . The chief began looking through the phone book, wondering as he did so if the Beijing high-flyer was as bright as he'd thought. "Inspector" Wang probably spent all his time behind a desk. And it was a known fact that cities rotted the brain.

Mr. Chu, former owner of the calligraphy, was a wiry man with a pinched face and sharp, calculating eyes. He greeted the inspector with half a smile and led him into the sitting room.

"Have a seat," said Chu. "This sofa is new. It cost me two thousand yuan."

Wang sat down. It wasn't even comfortable.

"It's nice to see this case being handled at a higher level," Chu—he reminded Wang of a rat—went on. "The thief got away with a lot, you know."

"Yes, I know. I—"

"The hi-fi was the latest design. CD, Full graphic equalization, twin cassette decks and Dolby noise reduction. All miniaturized. And Japanese, of course. That's four thousand yuan, full price, though I got a good deal out of the retailer. You can, you know, if you take the right line with them. Can I offer you some tea?"

"Er, no, thanks."

"Are you sure? I'm having some."

"No, that's fine."

The rat-man shouted an order into the kitchen.

"What about the calligraphy scroll?" Wang asked.

"That was the wife's."

As if on cue, a woman entered and handed Chu a mug of tea. He took it without a word of thanks. "The inspector asked about your scroll," he told her instead. "The one that was stolen. The one they say was worth money."

Mrs. Chu looked down at the floor.

"It looked a very nice piece," said Wang.

She said nothing.

"A little shy, my wife can be," said Chu.

"Qing dynasty, was it?" Wang went on.

The woman smiled and nodded.

"And valuable?" said Wang.

"She said it was," Chu cut in. "Can't see why. You can hardly read it."

"What period was it? Guangxu Emperor?"

"Not sure," said Mrs. Chu.

"I hope you get it back. When you do, you should find out more about it. Er, how long had you had it for?"

"Long time," said Mrs. Chu.

"We paid virtually nothing for it," added her husband. "Bought it off Old Ting. Creepy Ting, people called him. He wasn't a businessman."

Wang nodded. He remembered Creepy Ting, a man who made Wang's current host seem a model of charm and humanity. Ting had been a keen supporter of Kang Sheng, the Shandong-born Party boss who had amassed a huge art collection during the Cultural Revolution by getting people like Ting to ransack the homes of families like the Xus. Ting was known to have ransacked rather more works of art than he sent to his master—but after 1976 he had fallen on hard times, and had been forced to sell his ill-gotten collection at the low prices then prevailing.

"That's the secret of all success in business," Mr. Chu went on. "Buy cheap, sell dear. Simple when you know how." He looked round, as if at an imaginary, applauding audience, then turned to his visitor. "Now, Inspector, tell me what you intend to do to catch these thieves. I expect to hear something positive: in my view the forces of law and order have become remarkably slack in the last few years!"

Wang thought of the last case he had been on, and the fight he had had with three knife-wielding Triad thugs, and gave a weary nod.

4

Wang and Rosina dined alone again.

"So how did you get on at the police station?" said Rosina.

"All right. Nothing special."

"Oh," Rosina replied, then took another mouthful of bean-curd cheese. "Nothing more than that?"

"No."

"Ah." Another mouthful. "They were really nice down at the clinic. I, er, said I'd go and give a talk there on nursing in a modern city hospital. You don't mind, do you?"

"Why should I?"

"Because I asked you to keep away from police matters. It's hypocritical of me."

"No. It's fine. I didn't know you liked giving speeches."

"It's a talk, not a speech. To fellow professionals. Well, a nurse and two assistants. But they use a lot of interesting techniques here, you know. Traditional medicine. It's cheaper, and the locals believe in it."

"That's good."

"In fact, I'd like to spend some time there, looking at

their work. I thought it would be a good way of getting to know some Nanping people.''

"Yes.'' Wang took a piece of curd.

"I told them about the figwort,'' said Rosina. "They were all interested. The nurse said we must do something to protect it. Apparently there's a plan to flood Snake Valley.''

Wang looked puzzled.

"They want to build a series of dams and create reservoirs for irrigation, fish-farming and hydroelectricity.''

"That's ambitious . . . But why not? Fresh fish is unobtainable round here. And there's a terrible energy shortage.''

"It's crazy. It'll cost a fortune. All those fields, and your memorial, would vanish.''

"The village has to progress economically—''

"Anyone with any intelligence is against it! Supposing it doesn't work? Supposing the dam leaks or the fish die or the lake silts up? Supposing it just doesn't make money? Fei Baoren—she's the nurse—reckons that Secretary Wu is after the kickbacks he'll get from awarding construction contracts.''

Wang frowned. "Father always said Wu was a good man.''

"People can change,'' Rosina replied. "Or maybe your father misread him?''

Silence fell.

"Anming has a couple of fields in Snake Valley,'' said Wang after a pause. "I take it Secretary Wu intends paying people for the fields he floods?''

"I don't know,'' Rosina replied.

Wang sighed gloomily. "Even if he does, Anming's useless with money. You can't drink fields . . .''

"You'd better go and talk to him.''

"Yes, I suppose I should.''

"Of course you should. He needs help, Anzhuang.''

The door of Courtyard Four creaked open. This time Anming himself was behind it. He appeared to be sober.

"Hello, Anzhuang," said the older man quietly.

Wang smiled and held out a hand, upon which his brother smiled. "Come in."

The inspector crossed the courtyard and entered the bed/sitting room he had sneaked a view of yesterday. Anming had made a small effort at tidying up—the piles of books had been squared off, the papers strewn across the floor had been cleared away—but there was just too much clutter for the place ever to look anything other than a mess.

"Tea?"

"Please," Wang replied, hoping it wouldn't be local.

Anming went into his kitchen and Wang gazed round at the bedsit. Books. Father had always told them to read as much as they could. Folders full of notes. Anming should have been a teacher, only he had never been able to concentrate on anything for long. A family photo from about 1963: Granny Peng, Mother, Father (looking so old), the three children. Wang wondered whether this always had pride of place up there on the dresser, or whether it had been specially positioned in the last few days.

Anming reappeared with the tea. "Here we are. We grow it locally, you know."

"Thanks."

He sat down. "Look, I'm sorry about, er, the other night. Those banquets are all the same. A toast to this, a toast to that—before you know where you are, you're full of that *Maotai* stuff and it, well, takes over."

"That's OK."

"And I guess I should have asked you both round here. I can't wait to meet Rosina." He paused. "The old place is a bit untidy at the moment. We'll have a banquet at Zhou's Noodle House: Old Zhou's still running it, you know. Only he's put his prices up recently . . ."

"We'd rather visit you here."

Anming grinned. "You won't mind the clutter?"

"Of course not."

"That's settled then. Let's fix a day."

They did so. Wang took a sip of tea. He didn't want to be too direct . . .

"Still reading a lot, then, I see."

"Oh, yes. Classics mainly, of course—but factual stuff, too. One has to keep up to date."

Wang took a book off a pile. "Land law."

"Yes. I was thinking of studying law. China needs lawyers. Under the old system the police could just . . ." Anming's voice died away. "How's our sister?"

"Busy, as ever."

"Earning lots of money, I'm sure."

"Much more than you or I will ever have."

"You still have your privileges."

Wang thought of the jeep-ride to the village. "Some. But you know how it is nowadays. Money's talking louder and louder. Which is why we need to discuss your land."

"Ah. That's why you're here. You know what's happening, don't you?"

"Tell me."

Anming told Wang what he had already learnt from Rosina. Plus some information about compensation.

"It's not enough. Two thousand yuan. What the hell can you get with that nowadays?"

Wang thought: if each bottle costs one yuan fifty . . .

"Wu says the fish-farm is a village project," Anming went on. "He says everyone will benefit from it. He says that he needs to keep costs down, and that anyone who tries to argue the compensation up is putting personal interest above the general good. He says we're saboteurs, reactionaries."

"How many other people are there in your situation?"

"Enough. We've formed a group. We're fighting."

"Hence the book on land law?"

Anming looked ashamed. "At first, yes. But I've really got interested in it. I'd like to know more. Study it properly . . ."

Wang remembered his brother saying exactly the same thing in 1967 about Mao Zedong Thought. Then in the late seventies about science and technology; then in the late eighties about market economics.

"If I got a decent payment out of Wu, I could go on a

law course,'' Anming continued. ''Jinan TV University do one. But I'd need a video recorder, textbooks, time off work . . .'' He pointed to a pile of books. ''Justice. Dad always talked about justice, didn't he? Maybe, if I could become a lawyer, I could help bring it about . . . But I won't if that bastard Wu nails me down over the land, will I?''

Fei Baoren arrived at the guesthouse as arranged. She paused on the verandah—which door had Rosina said? Left? She knocked, and got no answer. Right, then, it must be.

''Hi. Come in.'' Rosina was ready, in walking shoes and slacks. ''Let's go.''

''It's everywhere,'' Rosina explained to her fellow nurse as they climbed the hill. ''Just growing wild. I'm sure money could be made from it. It's another argument you could use against Secretary Wu's fish-farm.''

''So you really are on our side?'' Baoren asked.

''Yes.''

''Despite . . .'' She didn't complete the sentence, but didn't need to.

''Despite my social position? I'm on your side because I happen to believe you're right.''

Baoren smiled. ''Most people round here think the project is wonderful. More money, that's all they see: they don't understand the costs.''

''That's old thinking,'' said Rosina.

Baoren winced.

''People in Beijing are becoming more and more aware of the environment,'' Rosina added.

Baoren winced again. They reached the top of the pass and began to walk down Snake Valley.

''These fields will be fine,'' said Baoren once they had rounded the first corner. ''Wu wouldn't dare flood them. They're prime land, and they belong to the top families.'' Then, further down: ''This land will all vanish. That bit over there belongs to us—well, we have the right to cultivate it, anyhow.'' Baoren pointed to a fenced-off plot marked PRIVATE. ''That sign is my father's protest,'' she

explained. "He says either people have rights over land or
they don't: if we do, then the Communist Party shouldn't
intimidate us into selling."

Rosina nodded. "Who's actually buying? Secretary
Wu?"

"The fish-farm cooperative. Which is run by the Party.
Which is run by Secretary Wu, who decides on things like
construction contracts. And that's where the kickbacks
come in."

It was Rosina's turn to wince. What would Anzhuang
say?

They reached the small path to the memorial. Rosina led
the way up to the trees. "See, it's growing everywhere."

Baoren pulled out a figwort plant and examined the root.
"All my life I've lived in Nanping, and I've never noticed
this. That shows how interested I am in Revolutionary heroes . . . We should gather some samples."

The women set to work. It was a pleasant day, and Rosina soon found herself immersed in the task. Above her
head, a skylark was warbling. A rivulet babbled somewhere
nearby; in the distance, a water-pump chugged—

The cough came from a clump of trees no more than
twenty metres away, followed at once by a curse and the
sound of someone charging through undergrowth. Rosina
stood up, ran a few steps in pursuit then stopped.

"He was spying on us!" she exclaimed.

"You don't know that," Baoren replied defensively.

"What else was he doing? The way he ran off . . ."

Baoren looked pained. "My opposition to this project is
unpopular. Associate with me, and you'll become unpopular too."

"I'll decide with whom I associate," Rosina replied.
"We'll carry on collecting until we have enough speci-
mens, then return home."

"Ganbei!" said Rosina. "To our harvest!"

"To our harvest!" Baoren replied. They clinked tea
mugs and drank.

They were celebrating their discovery in the Chrysanthe-

mum Tea House, a small local restaurant with formica-
covered tables, wooden benches and whitewashed walls. A
cassette player blasted out pop hits from Guangzhou: the
only other customer, an old man slurping noodles in the far
corner, couldn't eavesdrop even if he wanted to.

"You should meet my father," said Baoren. "You'll like
him, I know. He's a sensitive man—and he's had to put
up with a lot in his life, just because of his background.
Rich peasant, they classified him as. They treated him terribly for thirty years as a result. And they still haven't
'taken the class hats off' yet. I often wonder how he lived
through it all—and kept his self-respect, his gentleness."

Rosina nodded.

"I suffered, too, of course," Baoren went on. "But the
worst persecutions—the vandalism, the cowshed, the jet-
plane rides—were over by the time I was growing up. I got
some education; I got taken on at the clinic—they had to,
I knew that bloody 'Barefoot Doctor's Manual' cover to
cover." She suddenly looked bitter. "Even so, for the first
few years the Party seemed to think I was only waiting for
my first chance to poison them."

"The Party?"

"Wu, Yao, that old witch of a wife of his—*Aiya*, what
am I saying? They're probably all friends of yours; they
probably gave a huge banquet to welcome you . . ."

"I don't come that cheap," Rosina said firmly.

"No. I'm sorry." Baoren sucked the last drop from her
mug and called to the restaurant owner for refills of boiling
water. "Have you tried the local tea?" she asked, as the
owner looked up from his abacus and shuffled over—
shuffled perhaps because Baoren was unpopular, perhaps
because this was a traditionally male establishment, or perhaps because he was plain lazy.

"No."

"Don't. It's revolting."

The water was poured and the restaurateur went back to
his sums.

"Didn't you ever want to leave Nanping?" Rosina
asked.

Baoren sighed. "Of course. But I'm the only child. My mother died when I was a baby, and Father never remarried. It was even harder for rich-peasant categories to find partners then than it is now, and that's saying something." A look of self-pity crossed Baoren's face for a moment, then was gone. She could not afford such indulgences. Rosina's admiration for her grew.

"I'll pay: you're my guest," said Baoren when the bill arrived. Rosina watched her produce a simple grey purse and pull out some grubby notes. Then they got to their feet and left.

The restaurant's one other customer appeared to take no notice of their leaving until they were out of sight, whereupon he stood up, muttered something to the owner, and began to follow them.

5

Baoren and her father, Fei Zhaoling, lived in a compound on the outskirts of the village. It was reached by a long muddy path that led at first between high walls then out across small, old-fashioned chessboard fields.

"We have to share our home," Baoren told Rosina, as they crossed a stream and came in sight of the dark brick walls. "They moved in two poor peasant families back in the fifties; now we've just got the Lus in the west rooms—the Tais got so rich they built themselves a house on the hillside. Fat chance of us ever having that kind of money."

Rosina nodded sympathetically.

"Old Lu was on the Neighbourhood Committee," Baoren went on. "One of his jobs was to spy on us. Reports, once a month."

"That's terrible."

Baoren shook her head. "Everyone with a rich-peasant or landlord background suffered the same. And Old Lu was only doing what he was told. He never lied about us, like a lot of vigilantes did. And when I went for that job at the clinic, he even put in a report saying I was of good character."

Baoren led the way up a stone-flagged path and reached

for a key. "That's my room, there," she said, pointing across to a bright-curtained window. She smiled. "It's crazy: people are coining in money now, yet I feel really privileged to have a room of my own. Can you believe that? 'Four bare walls,' and I feel like a princess."

They crossed to the main, northern door, and entered a tidy but poverty-haunted room. No carpet, two wooden chairs, a bare bulb. Not even a TV or a Chinese-made cassette player. On a shelf was a photograph, not as one might have expected of family ancestors, or even of Baoren's dead mother, but of Baoren herself. Beneath it, a stocky middle-aged man in a blue denim jacket and grey nylon trousers was sitting reading a magazine. He got slowly to his feet.

"Father, this is Lin Xiangyu," Baoren began.

Fei Zhaoling looked at the new arrival suspiciously. 'Yes?"

"She's interested in our campaign—"

"Is she? In what way?"

Baoren told her father about the figwort, and about Rosina's more general enthusiasm for environmental matters.

"From Beijing, eh?" he said at the end.

"That's right," Baoren replied proudly.

"Hmph! Well, we don't need help from outside." Fei Zhaoling scowled. "I appreciate your interest—but if you're visiting, I'd stick to the scenery. Enjoy it while it's still here."

"Father!"

"It's a Nanping matter, and should be sorted out by Nanping people."

"But Rosina is—" Baoren began, then fell silent.

"What is she?"

"Very concerned," said Baoren.

"The more concern outside well-wishers show, the more concern outside authorities take. Thank you for your interest, Lin Xiangyu, but we must fight this battle ourselves." Then he sat down and began reading his magazine again, as if Rosina had vanished into thin air.

•   •   •

She told Wang the story from the beginning and in great detail, then suddenly she was in tears.

"Poor Baoren," she said. "Tied to a rude old bastard like that."

"It's her life. You said yourself, she chose to stay here."

"I guess so." She turned to her husband. "All those horrible things that happened in the past . . ."

"They happened all over China," said Wang.

"Yes. I know." Rosina dried her eyes, and Wang took her in his arms, overcome with pity and affection. After a long, long hug, Rosina whispered something in his ear.

"In the middle of the afternoon?" Wang said. Then he thought, why not? He started to take off his jacket—

There was a knock at the door.

"*Aiya!*"

There was another knock, then a third.

Wang crossed to the door and opened it. A young woman walked in.

"Hello. You must be Wang Anzhuang. I'm Fei Baoren. I came to apologize to your wife. I expect she's told you what happened."

Rosina, who was sitting on the bed, stood up.

"I'm so sorry," said Baoren. "It's not at all like him."

"That's OK," Rosina replied. "I don't blame you." The two women suddenly walked towards each other and embraced.

"Tea?" said Wang, retiring to the bathroom where there was a Thermos and some mugs.

Baoren looked flustered. "Now I've embarrassed your husband. Typical: I always make a mess of things."

"I'm sure you—"

"I'm inept socially. I don't mix much: the daughter of a rich-peasant category is still not someone to be seen with."

"Not nowadays, surely?"

"Of course. In Beijing, I'm sure, it's different. If you're intelligent and able, you can get on in life. Meet interesting people—people who read and think and do things. Here . . ."

Wang re-entered with mugs of tea. "Not the local product, I'm afraid," he said.

"That's fine," Baoren replied.

"You dislike it?"

"I hate it."

"So do I. Now, tell me about your protest group . . ."

"I like her," said Wang, once their visitor had left, after a long and impassioned monologue about ecology, to prepare dinner back home.

Rosina smiled.

"She acts according to her conscience," Wang went on. "I respect that. Is she married?"

"No."

"She's thirty."

"I was twenty-nine when you married me."

"That's Beijing. This is the countryside: if you're not married by the time you're—well, it was twenty when I was a lad . . ."

Rosina shook her head. "Sometimes I hate the Party," she said, after a pause.

Wang winced. "I know."

"They've done that to her. Your father's friends. It's not right."

"No," Wang said in a low voice. "You have to understand how bad things were before the Revolution . . ." he began, but his heart wasn't in it. "Let's do what we were going to do before we were interrupted," he said instead.

Wang was awoken by a knock at the door.

"Dinnertime already?" he muttered.

"Inspector Wang!"

"Who is it?"

"Mrs. Ming. I have a message for you. From Party Secretary Wu."

"Oh. Hold on a minute."

He pulled on a pair of trousers and a shirt that seemed to have buttons in all the wrong places, and opened the door. The landlady cast a critical eye over him, then spoke:

"The Secretary has just telephoned me. He wants you to go and see him tonight."

"Oh."

"He'll send a car. At eight o'clock. And you're to come alone."

Wang was puzzled, but too dopey to express that puzzlement. "Thank you, Mrs. Ming."

The VW Shanghai pulled up by the high white walls of Secretary Wu's villa. Wang got out, watched the driver turn the car then lit a Panda cigarette, which he smoked wondering what the local Party boss wanted to see him about so urgently.

The recent robberies? Station Chief Huang seemed to be doing as much as he could, given his limited resources.

The fish-farm? Perhaps Wu wanted some advice. What would your father have done? A nice thought. But why so suddenly; why right now?

A thought struck him: that there was a hidden microphone in their room, and that Mrs. Ming had heard Rosina's disloyal comments about the Party. A momentary chill of primal terror ran through him: the ghost of the Zedong Emperor will never quite leave those who lived through his reign. Then the inspector composed himself: that sort of thing doesn't go on nowadays. Well, not often, anyway. More likely the Secretary wanted some business favour done via contacts Wang might have in Beijing. Wu was probably in the middle of some transaction and needed help straight away.

The inspector took a drag, recalled the most recent Party circular on smoking—"members who cannot quit this unhealthy habit are reminded that the last third of the cigarette is the most poisonous"—then smoked his Panda down to the stub. The last third is also the best. Then he opened Wu's iron gate and made his way up the path to the Secretary's front door.

As he rang the bell, Wang cast a quick eye over the main lock. Wu clearly thought that nobody would dare rob a Party Secretary.

The door opened. "Come in!"

After the vulgarity of Mr. Chu's villa, Secretary Wu's home was a welcome contrast. There was a simple hallway; the sitting room contained a few pieces of mahogany furniture, a rug in the middle and scrolls of calligraphy or classical landscapes on the walls. Nice stuff, especially that river with the boats on. Wu pointed to a chair beneath a shelf with a marble bust of Karl Marx on it, and bade his guest sit down. There was a coldness in his voice that did not suit the occasion or the surroundings. And no offer of refreshment—very inhospitable. What was going on? Wu began to speak:

"Inspector Wang—when we welcomed you to Nanping, we did so in good faith. Your father was a man of outstanding integrity and loyalty. You had a good record of service to the country, both in the People's Liberation Army and the Public Security Bureau. We thought—well, never mind what we thought. It seems we were wrong. We are bitterly disappointed in your conduct. I'm afraid I must ask you and your wife to leave the village as soon as possible."

Wang was so taken aback that he couldn't find any words.

"You know what I'm talking about," the Secretary went on.

"No . . ."

Secretary Wu shrugged. "If you have business to conclude here, do so in the next two days. If you and your wife are not out of the vicinity by Friday at ten hundred hours, I shall contact your superiors in Beijing and lodge a formal complaint. I shall do the same if you have any further dealings with subversive elements in our village. Naturally, you cease to be the guest of the local Party as from now. I don't know what the tourist rates are at the guesthouse; you'd better ask Mrs. Ming tomorrow morning." He paused. "That's all I have to say. You can go now."

Wang got slowly to his feet. "Subversive . . . ?" he said feebly. "Don't you remember who I am?"

"An outsider. A visitor. Now, I'm expecting further company this evening, so I'd be grateful if you would

leave. Once again, I must say how disappointed I am that
you have abused our hospitality. Goodbye, Inspector.''

"I don't know how you can—"

"The driver will take you back."

Wang stared at his host for a moment. Then he turned
and walked out of the room, the house and the compound.

The car was waiting.

"I'm walking," Wang told the driver.

The Shanghai followed him a short way down the road,
like one of these new private taxis touting for a fare, then
backed off, possibly because the prospective passenger told
him to go to hell.

Wang slept badly and rose early next morning. He went
and sat on the verandah, looking over the roofs of his former home village and listening to the sounds as it stirred
for another working day.

He had no idea how much their room would cost a tourist, but he'd pay. And he was damned if he was moving
out on Friday. Secretary Wu could complain as much as he
liked: Beijing wouldn't take any notice of a jumped-up provincial nobody. It would go down on his record, of course,
but so what?

Keeping a clean record means a lot.

Not as much as keeping face. Wang would leave when
he felt like it, and not a moment before. And when he got
back to the capital, he'd make sure Wu's fish-farm never
got beyond the planning stage.

Aiya . . . He knew he was being petty, but he couldn't
help it. His father had worked himself to an early grave for
these people; now one of them had insulted his wife and
another insulted him. Bloody peasants.

The door opened. Rosina was beside him. She put an
arm round his waist and rested her head against his shoulder: last night she'd said sorry over and over again and
cried tears of regret—none of which Wang required of her.

A pheasant's-tail of dust from the valley announced that
a vehicle was approaching. A police motorcycle. Station
Chief Huang, no doubt eager to tell his superior officer that

he wasn't welcome at his station any more. Wang determined that Huang should enjoy this experience as little as possible.

The bike came to a halt and the chief got off. He looked flustered. Good.

"Inspector!"

"Yes."

"You must come! Quickly!"

"Why?"

"Because—you must. There's been another robbery."

"So?"

"They got it wrong. The victim was at home. They killed him."

Wang wanted to give a shrug—always a rude gesture in China—and say it wasn't his business any longer, what a terrible shame he had to go and he hoped the station chief and his men would soon solve the crime. But he didn't.

"Who was it?" he asked instead.

"Wu. Secretary Wu."

6

The scene was depressingly familiar. Papers strewn across the floor, rectangles of dust on the walls where Wu's paintings had been, and in the middle of it all, a man lying face down on a rug in a pool of dried black blood.

The Beijing detective pulled on a pair of rubber gloves, bent down over the body and lifted an arm. It was stiff. The parts in contact with the floor had become purplish, the upward-facing parts cream-coloured. Wang pressed his fingers into one of the lower parts, watched what happened and nodded.

"Lividity's pretty fixed," he said.

"I noticed that," said Station Chief Huang. He wrote "lividity fixed" in his notebook.

"Rigor's pretty complete, too," Wang went on.

"Naturally. Rigor . . . complete . . ."

"Got a thermometer?"

"Er . . ."

"Body temperature's the best informal time-of-death indicator. I think my wife's got one back at the guesthouse. In the meantime, let's get a proper crime-scene description. Nothing's been touched?"

"Of course not."

"And a photographer's on his way?"

"Of course." The chief made a note to phone for one as soon as possible.

Wang looked around the room and began scratching his head.

"It's obvious though, isn't it?" the chief went on.

"No."

"Thieves."

"I thought your thieves were after electrical goods. Wu doesn't appear to have had any. Apart from that ancient TV and a radiogram, neither of which were portable or worth much."

"Well, they must have thought he had stuff worth stealing. Then they got here, realized there wasn't much, took down the art—then were surprised by the Secretary!"

Wang kept on scratching his head. "You also said they always made sure a house was empty before entering it."

"Well, yes. But they must have made a mistake this time. Wu must have been working late—he often did, you know—and have fallen asleep at his desk."

"The office light would have been on."

"They would have thought it had been left on for security. People are doing that a lot now, since the robberies."

Wang made a note to check how easy it was to see into the office from outside.

"The kitchen window was smashed," the chief continued. "That's typical of the other robberies."

"One mustn't jump to conclusions. We—I mean you—should get on with interviewing all possible witnesses. Secretary Wu's driver, anyone seen in the area, people who saw Wu shortly before his death. You can start with me."

The chief looked genuinely shocked. *"You?"*

"I was here for about ten minutes last night. Secretary Wu invited me over."

"Oh."

"Let's say from ten past eight to twenty past."

"Ah."

"He just wanted a brief chat. During which he said that

he was expecting further company. I think that further company was the killer.''

The chief shook his head. "The Secretary was very choosy about who he allowed to enter his house. One reason being that he didn't want people to know what was in here. You were quite honoured, you know, to be invited.''

"Who else shared this honour?''

"Senior Party members: Deputy Yao or his wife, Factory-manager Wei, Cui Shaobing, er, myself.''

"Who's Cui Shaobing?''

"Head of Agriculture. He lives a few houses away.''

Wang said the name to himself, committing it to memory, then nodded. "Did Wu have a lover?''

The chief looked shocked again. "The Secretary was a model of Socialist morality!''

Possible mistress, Wang thought. The sound of a siren became audible: soon after, two men in white coats and round white caps entered, and rolled the body on to a stretcher. One of them looked round at the room with a ghost of a grin on his face. Rich bastard, he was probably thinking. The other man, his senior, handed the chief a form to sign.

"Where are you taking him?'' Wang asked.

"Wentai,'' the man replied.

The inspector nodded. He would have preferred them to take Wu to Jinan, the state capital, rather than the local county town. But what could he do? He consoled himself with the thought that any doctor should be able to ascertain that the victim had been hit over the left temple with a heavy object—almost undoubtedly the bust of Marx, which had gone missing. A proper time of death would be established. They would find out if there were other wounds. They would check things like nail-scrapings and fibres from Wu's clothes. In Beijing, of course—

Secretary Wu left his house for the last time feet-first beneath a white blanket. Wang watched him depart, then turned to his local colleague. "You're setting up an incident HQ, I take it?''

"Of course.''

"Where?"

"Er, here."

"In this room?"

"No. Upstairs."

The chief led the way up to the landing, and tried various doors. A big bedroom; a smaller bedroom—both beds made up, neither slept in. Wu's office, which needed to be sealed off and searched. A boxroom, virtually empty.

"Here, of course," he said.

"Do you want me to assist with the interviews?"

Station Chief Huang looked doubtful, then nodded. "In an advisory capacity, of course."

"Of course."

"Driver Gao," said Huang, "tell me about your movements from, let's say, six o'clock yesterday evening."

The interviewee pondered. "Six o'clock? Well, I must have driven the Secretary back from his office about then. Then I cleaned and checked the car—he was very particular about maintenance; he said the car belonged to the People, and should be kept in tip-top condition. Then I went home and watched TV with my wife and child. At a quarter to eight, I drove to the guesthouse, collected Inspector Wang and brought him over here. Shortly afterwards, the inspector left the villa. He declined a lift, impolitely, I must say, so I put the car away and walked home. I watched a little more TV, then went to bed."

The chief nodded. "Did you see anyone about, while you were waiting for the inspector or on your final trip back home?"

"No. You know how quiet it is up here after about seven."

"You saw no one?"

"I saw two men walking up the hill when I was on my way to the guesthouse. And another fellow on his own, walking towards the villas."

"Ah. Can you give descriptions?"

"I was concentrating on the road. The two together looked quite smart. And middle-aged. The one on his own—I can't say. He wasn't acting suspiciously, just . . . walking.''

"Slow or fast?" Wang cut in.

"I don't know. Ordinary speed. Maybe a bit quick, but he wasn't running or anything.''

"What did he look like? Height? Build? Age? Clothes?"

The driver winced. "Quite tall. Build? Don't know. Ordinary. And I didn't see his face, so I don't know his age. Thirty? Forty? Not a kid, but not old, either. I can't remember what he was wearing. Just ordinary trousers and a sweater, I guess. And a cap of some kind.''

Wang made some notes. "And what time was this?"

"About ten to eight."

"Right." Wang turned to the chief. "Sorry. Carry on."

Huang smiled at the apology, then tried to think of some more questions. "I think we've covered the ground satisfactorily," he said at length. "Any supplementary questions, Inspector?"

"Yes," said Wang. The local man looked a bit hurt, but nodded to him to go ahead. Which he did: "Driver Gao, do you know if Secretary Wu was intending to see anyone else that evening?"

"No."

"You had no orders to collect anyone?"

"No. Only you."

"And he didn't mention anyone?"

"No."

"Did he often receive visitors that late?"

"When necessary. The Secretary always put the public good above personal convenience."

"I'm sure. What kind of mood was he in when you last saw him?"

"Happy—he seemed happy. That was unusual, as he'd been worried lately."

"Do you know what that worry was about?"

"I think so. He'd had threats. From Weipowan. About the fish-farm."

"What sort of threats?"

"I don't know. Unpleasant ones. Those fuckers . . ."

Wang nodded. The two villages were old rivals: he remembered getting in fights with lads from Weipowan for no reason other than that rivalry. (Anming had got into similar fights, too, and Wang had usually had to rescue him.) Add to this the fact that Weipowan, at the end of Snake Valley, stood to get flooded if one of Secretary Wu's dams burst, and it was hardly surprising that its residents weren't too keen on the plan.

"They were definitely from Weipowan?" he asked nevertheless.

"That's what the Secretary said. And I'm sure he was right. Nanping people loved the Secretary. He looked after us. I know there's all this talk nowadays about officials being gold and jade on the outside and rotten cotton within, but he wasn't like that. He worked for us, day and night . . ."

The driver seemed on the edge of tears. Wang let him hang his head and pretend to have a slight cold—common, this time of year—then carried on with his questioning.

"Do you have any idea why Secretary Wu was suddenly happier yesterday evening?"

"No."

"None at all?"

"No. Unless it was something to do with you, Inspector." There was an accusatory tone in the driver's voice.

"That's always possible," Wang said calmly. "Is there anything else you want to say?"

"No."

Mrs. Ou was Wu's cook and housekeeper: Wang remembered her as a fit, healthy middle-aged woman; now she was in her seventies, and looked it.

"I made rice and bean-curd for the Secretary," she told Station Chief Huang in a thin, frightened voice, "which he ate, well, I suppose about half past six. Then he went to his office to work—the one upstairs, I mean, not his one in Nanping."

"D'you know what sort of work?" Wang asked her.

"Party work, I'm sure, Inspector. The Secretary always

put the interests of the People before his own.''

"And what kind of mood was he in when you served him dinner?"

"Quite good. It was so nice to see." She began shaking her head.

"Any idea why?"

"I've no idea. Maybe no reason. A man who has done so much for the People shouldn't need reasons to be happy—oh, excuse me, Comrade Inspector.'' She pulled a handkerchief out of the pocket of her old Mao jacket and snuffled into it. "Your father always said Wu was his ideal successor, Comrade Inspector. He would have been so pleased to see everything the Secretary achieved.'' Another snuffle, and some tears.

"You keep the bed in the spare room made up, I see," said Wang, once she had recovered.

"Yes," Mrs. Ou replied, managing a look of pride.

"Who for?"

"Weidong. He comes to stay whenever they have business to discuss."

"Weidong?"

"The Secretary's son." Mrs. Ou smiled, then suddenly looked horrified. "He wasn't here last night, though."

"You know that?"

"Yes. He only left a couple of days ago. He has to come all the way from Jinan; he'd never be back so soon."

"But the bed was still ready, just in case?"

"It's always ready. Weidong loved his father, Comrade Inspector. He was, well, a little wayward, but he was a good lad really. Deep down inside." The handkerchief came out again, and this time the tears wouldn't stop.

Station Chief Huang was staring at the ceiling. "Interesting interviews, but nothing material emerging from them, in my view."

"Nothing material? There was all that stuff about the Secretary's son Wu Weidong!"

The local policeman shook his head. "Wu Weidong is not the sort of person to commit a crime."

"How do you know?"

"I know my criminal types."

"What work does he do?"

"I'm not sure. Something for the municipality in Jinan."

"Does he possess a motorbike, or anything that could get from Jinan to here and back in an evening?"

"He has a car."

"A car!" Wang didn't even dream of owning a car, an item that costs a lifetime's salary for an honest official.

"A blue Toyota. And everyone round here knows it. He could never sneak in here unnoticed."

"Driver Gao said the area was deserted after seven."

"It is. But the only way to get here from Jinan is straight up the main street, where there's always someone about. If Wu Weidong came to this house yesterday evening, someone in Nanping will know."

"Good. I'm sure you'll be getting men on to that. Then there's the threats Gao mentioned—"

"Wu often got them. People in office do. You're not taking them seriously, are you?"

"The recipient is dead . . . Then there's Secretary Wu's change of mood. We don't know what he was depressed about—maybe it wasn't the notes. Then something cheered him up. What? I regret to say it wasn't me. We had a, er, difference of opinion. So I guess it was to do with whoever was coming after me. You're sure he didn't have a mistress?"

"Positive."

"Was there any colleague whose visit he would particularly be looking forward to? A particular friend?"

"The Secretary kept his distance from people. That's the best way for an official to be, in my view."

"And what about the rest of his family?"

"Wu Weidong is the only member he ever saw. His ex-wife and daughter live in Qingdao. They have no contact with him, and haven't for years." The chief paused, then added: "Mind if I ask you a question?"

"No."

"What did you and the Secretary talk about last night?"

Wang smiled. His colleague was quite right to ask him. And he should tell the truth—but that might create complications. "Old times. The Cultural Revolution. I'm afraid I get angry when I think of all the damage that got done."

"Secretary Wu did his best to counteract ultra-leftism," said the chief, scribbling something in a notebook. "Now, I must get a preliminary report in by lunchtime. We need more men, as soon as possible." He paused. "I wonder if I could ask you a favour . . ."

"To stay and guard the house?"

"Yes. Please rest assured that the moment we have manpower up to appropriate levels—"

"No problem."

"Good. Thank you. Er, you won't touch anything, will you?"

"Of course not."

Wang listened to Station Chief Huang's boots on the path, the roar of Station Chief Huang's new Happiness motorbike, and, finally, the silence. He reminded himself of his promises, to Rosina and, just now, to Huang. Then he stood up to begin his examination of the house.

7

Wang stood in the doorway of Secretary Wu's front room. A chalked outline, the sour, shitty smell of death and a big black bloodstain were all that were left of the man.

"This wasn't a robbery," he muttered. There were no signs of a struggle, no signs of panic. The "theft" had been carried out afterwards, no doubt to make the local police think exactly what the local police *did* think. A trick which would probably end up with a thief being shot for murder, and a thief's family being stigmatized way beyond their deserts.

"You worked for this holiday," Wang told himself, then began a search of the house. First, a quick look round to make the acquaintance of the owner.

The reception room. A brief look at the papers on the floor yielded little: agricultural and economic reports (modern Party Headquarters get bombarded with paper). Wang looked at the walls: eight rectangles, eight missing works of art. True, art was worth money these days, but Station Chief Huang had been right about one thing—they wouldn't be easy to sell round here . . . He wandered into the kitchen, which was tidy but simple, then into a store-room, where the only extravagance was a washing-machine. It hadn't been plumbed in, and was currently being used for storing rice.

Upstairs was the boxroom—the boxes were empty—and the two bedrooms. There was a trace of luxury in the latter: Wu had not paid for the rosewood cabinet or the silk pillowcases on a Party Secretary's salary. But apart from them—some backhanders come unrequested and cannot be returned without giving offence—there was no sign of unearned wealth. Wang recalled the comments of Wu's staff. Gold and jade: the mandarin ideal that had sustained China's government for two and a half thousand years from Confucius to Comrade Liu Shaoqi.

Gold and jade are lifeless minerals: Wu had been a human being. So, despite his colleague's assurances, Wang searched the room for evidence of an affair. There was none, any more than there was evidence of any interest in sex—how often searches of single men's homes produced caches of magazines from Hong Kong or, among more discerning search victims, erotic classics like the *Golden Lotus* or Li Yu's *Carnal Prayer Mat*.

So it was on to the Secretary's office. This small but important room had one uncurtained window that looked out over the walled front garden and, beyond, the road. Wang sat down at the heavy rosewood desk and looked out at the world: he could no longer see the road, but by raising his head a fraction the top of the wall came into view. Anyone outside who was curious as to whether the office was occupied only needed to pull themselves up on to the wall for a moment. The inspector shook his head—if he needed convincing, that had done it—and took a key-pick from his pocket.

The desk opened easily.

A diary would have been the perfect find, with a named appointment for nine p.m. last night. No such luck. Instead, there was a neat pile of papers under a carved calligrapher's inkstone. Top of the pile: two notes, one to Station Chief Huang, the other to the guesthouse manager, Mrs. Ming.

"Concerning Wang Anzhuang and Lin Xiangyu (also

known as Rosina Wang). These individuals are no longer
welcome in Nanping . . .''

Before he knew what he was doing, Wang had crumpled
up the papers and shoved them into his pocket.

Destruction of state evidence. A serious offence.

He took the blotter that Wu had pressed on as well.

Beneath the two letters was an official-looking document
in a plastic cover. A tender, from Yap Seeow Construction
Company, Shanghai, to build a series of dams in Snake
Valley ''to international standards of quality.'' Wang nodded with approval—then saw the cost. A million yuan.
How could a small village begin to raise that kind of
money? Shaking his head, he moved on to a second, even
smarter tender beneath it. Sheng He Design and Building
Cooperative of Jinan wanted one and a quarter million.
Both documents were dated last month: there was no cor-
respondence attached to either of them.

Wang sat back and stared at the ceiling, shocked at the
magnitude of these figures. And intrigued. People killed for
much less than the standard go-between's commission on
either of these contracts. But how did this apply in this
case? He let various permutations run through his mind, till
the sound of a bicycle bell on the road outside brought him
back to the immediate task. Glancing at his watch, Wang
pressed on.

Beneath the contracts was a file marked ''Opposition,
Nanping.'' It contained notes on the main opponents of the
fish-farm. Among these were:

''WANG ANMING. Good class background, but of weak
character. Drink problem. Easily led.'' A copy of his work
attendance record from Wei's factory was attached, which
did not make good reading.

''FEI BAOREN. Bad class background. Intelligent, manip-
ulative, dangerous. See attached report.'' The report was of
the strict surveillance Baoren had been subjected to over a
period of months—including an attempt at sexual entrap-
ment, which had failed.

''You bastard,'' Wang muttered to himself. ''Father
never did anything like that . . .''

"FEI ZHAOLING. Bad class background. Deceptively quiet type. Core member of protest group. Watch carefully." This last instruction had a tick against it—leading, Wang wondered, to last night's farcical interview?

"WEI SHAOJIA. Manager of Nanping Village Industries. Appears to be objectively concerned about 'environment,' but real motive may be that he doesn't want a rival centre of economic activity in area. Placate."

The next file was "Opposition, Weipowan." This turned out to be full of letters complaining about the physical threat posed to the old rival village by Nanping's dam. Their tone varied from Confucian politeness to simple violence. Five of the latter were composed from characters, cut out from comics and neatly pasted on to sheets of writing paper.

Build those dams and you will die.

Wang put them in a line. The work of one person. None bore dates. Or, obviously, addresses: the envelopes with them gave away their place of origin.

You will die.

Maybe Wang's local colleague was right to ignore these. People who send hate-mail usually just mean to frighten, not kill. The dams were only in the planning stage, too, not "built"—and there was no escalation of tone in the letters, the way Wang would expect if the sender had in fact turned killer. Also, from what Station Chief Huang said, these weren't the first such missives the Secretary had received. Nasty, though.

That was the contents of the desktop. The desk also had three drawers, all with nice pickable locks. In the top one were sets of accounts from local cooperatives, including Nanping Village Industries: all seemed to be doing well. Then a file full of correspondence about the road to Wentai. Wu had been complaining about its state from 1980 onwards. A final letter, to Vice President Zhu, seemed to have worked: Nanping had got its tarmac lifeline eight years later. Well fought, Secretary Wu.

The second drawer contained domestic details—bills and so on. None revealed extravagance, and a pass-book from the Agricultural Bank of Shandong showed modest savings fluctuating undramatically. Unless there was a hidden hoard of gold—in the washing-machine?—Secretary Wu did not look worth killing for his cash. His house, of course, was a different matter.

The third drawer was empty but for a few sheets of writing paper, on which the Secretary had been practising his calligraphy. Here was a new Secretary Wu, a private, reflective man. He had copied out the characters *kan po hong chen*—one of those four-ideogram phrases so common in Chinese. This one meant literally "see through red dust"; figuratively it meant to cast one's vision beyond the material world. To be prepared for death? Or was the meaning more political: was the colour of that dust important? There were also two four-line poems, which Wang recognized as Tang dynasty.

"BEES" by Le Yin

Down on the plains and up in the mountains
They feast on nature's greatest glories.
But when the blooms of a hundred flowers have
    been turned to honey
Who is all this hard work for? And all this
    sweetness?

"SICK LEAVE" by Bo Quyi

Propped up on my pillows, my workplace is a
    world away,
I have seen no one for two days.
Now at last I understand that for the public servant
It is only when ill that tranquillity can be found.

The inspector nodded sympathetically as he read the last one, then remembered the crumpled notes in his pocket and swore.

But it wasn't professional to get personal. Wang put the poems back in the drawer, locked it—then heard a motorbike engine in the distance. He glanced at his watch again. *Aiya*, time's a policeman's worst enemy . . .

Deputy Yao sat in Secretary Wu's office, in Secretary Wu's chair, at Secretary Wu's desk. He picked up his old boss's pen, stared at it, then put it back again.

"He won't be coming back," he muttered. "Now it's all up to me." He shook his head. "I must carry on. I must run things as he did. Exactly. Now, what did the secretary do first thing after lunch?" The old deputy gazed round the room, then called out to the fellow in the front office—what was his name?—to ask him.

"Have a mug of green tea then go to the lavatory," Assistant Xia called back. Deputy Yao, in the next office, didn't see the twinkle of amusement in the young man's eye.

"Right. Well, I'll do the same. Did he make the tea himself?"

"Sometimes."

"Ah. About half the time? I'll make it today; you do it tomorrow. Where's the Thermos?"

The old deputy made the tea slowly, and deliberately: how many spoonfuls did Secretary Wu put in? How long did he leave it to infuse? Then there was a knock on the door.

"Someone to see you, Secretary," said Xia.

"Acting Secretary, please. Who is it?"

"Wang Anzhuang. That policeman from Beijing."

"Ah! Wang Jingfu's son. Show him in."

The young man did so.

Yao held out a hand. "Comrade Wang," he said, slipping back into old Party usage in a way that only old and unimportant people do nowadays. "Welcome. Sit down. You'll have some tea? Good. How can I help you?"

"I want to ask a few questions about Secretary Wu."

"Ah. A fine man. A true servant of the People."

"He had ambitious plans for Snake Valley."

"Oh, yes."

"What were they, exactly?"

Yao described to Wang the same scheme that Fei Baoren had described, but in such glowing terms as to make them seem two different projects.

"And what stage were these plans at? Had the contracts for the construction of the dams been awarded?"

Yao's look of millennial optimism faded. "I don't know," he said. "I'm afraid Secretary Wu didn't really discuss the matter with me. I've always been more involved in the political side of things."

"Whom did he discuss it with?"

"I don't know. His superiors in Wentai and Jinan, I suppose. Secretary Wu was a man of great energy, but he operated best on his own. With support from his Party colleagues, of course."

Wang nodded. "Of course. Do you know how the dams were going to be paid for?"

The veteran cadre sighed. "Secretary Wu was going to get some kind of loan organized: there are all sorts of banks and things around nowadays. Red capitalism! We must make these contradictions serve the People."

"But the loan details hadn't been finalized?"

"No. I don't think so. I don't know . . ." Yao grinned. "The matter will be discussed by the Party Committee and brought to a satisfactory conclusion at a suitable point at some time in the future!"

Wang took the hint and changed the subject. "Tell me—were the items stolen from the Party Secretary's house valuable?"

"I've no idea."

"But Secretary Wu was a wealthy man, wasn't he?"

"No!" Yao said loudly, adding a vigorous shake of his head. "His family were poor peasants. Like mine. And yours, Wang An—er—Inspector Wang. Secretary Wu never amassed wealth."

"He had a fine villa."

"He had the use of a fine villa. That house belongs to the Party."

"Ah." Wang paused for thought. "But his art . . ."

"That was bought years ago. That sort of thing was

cheap once. I wish I'd bought some—but I was never able to satisfy myself that art dating from the pre–Revolutionary era was entirely free of unwholesome influence.''

''No. So Wu was not a rich man?''

''I've said. He was a true Communist. Such a man does not desire wealth.''

Wang nodded. Give or take the odd silk pillowcase, rosewood cabinet and work of art, Wang had a feeling the deputy was right: Secretary Wu had not used his office for personal gain. So try another tack. ''Have there been any thoughts as to who might succeed him?''

''That's for the regional Party to decide.''

''Would you accept the job?''

''It should go to a younger person.''

''Ah. Like Secretary Wu's son?''

That vigorous headshake again. ''The successful candidate should be local and have a history of Party activism. Wu Weidong fails on both counts. Personally, I do not consider him to be the right type, anyhow. Do you know the fellow?''

''No. I'd like to meet him.''

Yao frowned. ''You'll do so on Sunday, at the Memorial Meeting. You and your wife have received invitations, I take it?''

''No.''

''*Aiya!* Wang Jingfu's son and daughter-in-law, not invited! You *are* invited. By me, personally, now. I'll tell, er, the young man outside to organize it.'' Yao wrung his hands. ''It's all been set up in rather a hurry, I'm afraid. Secretary Wu was in such good health . . .'' The old deputy sighed, then looked up at his visitor. ''May I ask you to compose a short tribute to read out? As a distinguished guest? Your father would have wanted that, I'm sure.''

Wang couldn't help smiling at the irony of this request. ''I'd be delighted.''

Mrs. Ming had a number for the hospital at Wentai. After several attempts, Wang got connected; after various false routings on its internal system, he found himself through to the pathology department.

"Chen here. To whom am I talking?"

"Wang Anzhuang, Inspector, CID."

"Oh," came the lazy reply.

"From Beijing."

"How can I help you, Inspector?"

"I want to know about the late Secretary Wu."

"Of course. First, I must say that we operate under difficult conditions here. Space, time and financial resources are all limited. Nevertheless, my colleagues and I have carried out a postmortem examination of the body this afternoon with great thoroughness. The report is at this very moment being typed."

"Can you fetch it and read it to me?"

"Fetch . . . ? Is it really . . . ? Yes, Inspector."

There was nothing startling. Wu had died from one blow from a blunt object, some time between nine and eleven on Wednesday evening. He hadn't been fighting: there were no other wounds, and the only substance on his hands was ink. (Wang reflected that was probably from writing the two letters about him and Rosina, and smiled—till he remembered he had to write a tribute to the man that evening.) Wu had probably turned to face his attacker, who was right-handed and quite strong, but had not had time to defend himself.

"I don't know what the object was," Dr. Chen went on. "It was roundish and had ridges of some kind on it."

Wang nodded. The Secretary's skull had been shattered by Karl Marx's sideburns. "What instructions have you received about the burial of the body?" he asked.

"The usual. Cremation. On Monday, I think."

"This is a murder case!"

"We lack the facilities here to preserve bodies indefinitely. And our report is very thorough, I can assure you, Inspector. What purpose would be served by delay? We have never made a mistake in a postmortem, and we haven't in this case. If you wish to view the body yourself, you are most welcome to do so. But we don't have the time to give you a guided tour.''

Wang smiled at the image—did all pathologists have this kind of humour, or just all the ones he'd met?—then pondered for a moment and shook his head.

''Thank you, Dr. Chen,'' he said and put down the receiver.

8

The Memorial Meeting for Secretary Wu was held in the main hall at Nanping Party HQ. The barrack-like room had seen many such occasions—including one for Wang's father twenty-eight years ago. The form of the ceremony hadn't changed much since then: there would be a series of speeches, listened to in deferential silence by mourners in carefully planned rows (cadres at the front, non-Party members at the back), then a meal at a separate venue, traditionally simple and vegetarian but nowadays as ostentatious as the deceased's family could make it.

Wang, near the front, stood with his body at attention, used to the position from his Army days and well prepared for the long wait before anything happened. His eyes were free to roam, however: he began reading the slogans on the traditional paper wreaths, some several feet across, that hung round the walls.

"Eager for the Public Good!"

"A Red Heart, Always Loyal to the Party!"

"Strong as Steel, Just, Impervious to Flattery!"

He sighed at the formality of these expressions. Then memories came back of a time when exactly similar words had filled his grief-stricken heart with almost unbearable pride. In 1965, a teenage boy had stood here and read them about his own father. He had made a promise to that man's spirit, to live and die for China and for Socialism. Had he kept it? He'd tried, that was sure.

Was it still worth keeping?

A noise like a typhoon announced that Deputy Yao was trying out the microphone by blowing into it. It began to whistle: the old man gave it an icy stare, which, together with some knob-twiddling from Assistant Xia at the back of the hall, reduced it to obedient silence. The deputy began to speak.

"Long live the Party! Long live the People! That was the motto of Wu Changyan, a man whose life bears comparison with that of the soldier Lei Feng."

Wang felt a rush of fury, then amusement: mediocre officials in Beijing repeated standard eulogies, why shouldn't they in Nanping? As the squadrons of isms marched past in exactly the same battle order as at the banquet, Wang's thoughts went back to 1965 again. More images of his father. "Be prepared to die for justice," the old revolutionary had once told his son, up at that memorial . . .

When Yao finished, he announced the next speaker, a representative from Party HQ in Jinan. This was the keynote speech. In the Mao era, just as in Imperial China, its contents would have determined the fate of Wu's family, even to the point of life or death. Now it would be reported in full in the local press, and excerpts would be copied on to scrolls and given to the principal mourners.

Progress.

The man from HQ began to speak. Secretary Wu had triumphed over adversity in the Revolution. He had played a major role in the movement for Land Reform. He had tried to serve Nanping even in the dark days of the Cultural Revolution . . .

The inspector's gaze left this owl-like official and began to scrutinize the people who shared the podium with him. Family members traditionally stood to the right of the microphone. The tall man with wire-rimmed glasses and a fine head of dark hair had to be Wu Weidong. His suit was black and shiny with big lapels, the latest fashion. His face was expressionless, as befitted the formality of the occasion. To one side of him stood a dumpy woman in heavy spectacles, a white nylon coat and skirt, popsocks and flat shoes; to the other, a female of striking beauty, in make-up, high heels and a short dress that did not befit the formality of the occasion. Wu Weidong's sister and Wu Weidong's wife? The frail old woman hunched in a chair was the Secretary's wife who was, Wang had been told that morning, dying of a degenerative disease.

The man from Jinan wound up his speech and retired to his position to the left of the mike, the place of honour. Yao announced the next speaker: Wu Weidong. There was a frisson of interest as the murdered man's son stepped forward and stooped to take the microphone in his big right hand.

"My father was a keen advocate of reform," Wu Weidong began listlessly. "He understood the value of hard work, that it should be rewarded. 'To grow rich through labour,' he would say, 'is honourable.' "

Wang studied the speaker's face. No emotion, just like the voice. But did that mean anything?

". . . The list of my father's public achievements is long. Few homes had electricity when he took over the leadership of the local Party. Sanitation was poor, output from the Agricultural Implements Factory low . . ."

Did you love the man we're mourning today, Wu Weidong? Or did you kill him? Or—policemen see stranger things—both?

"Those speeches!" said Rosina, half suppressing a yawn as they walked up the high street past a line of parked official cars. "Apart from yours, of course."

Wang grinned.

"It's not right," she went on. "People need to let emotions out; they need to work through their grief, not shut it in a box. Putting on a front like that doesn't do anyone any good."

Wang was still not convinced by Rosina's new Western

ideas, though she was often coming back from hospital telling him of some problem solved by putting them into practice. "You can't go weeping all over the place in public,"
he said. "Especially if you're a man!"

Rosina tutted and took his arm. "Look!" said Wang suddenly. "That must be Wu Weidong's car!"

"You're changing the subject," Rosina commented, but
followed her husband across to a blue Toyota and joined
him in peering through the windows. The interior was
clean, and, apart from some fashion magazines strewn
across the back seat, tidy.

"Twenty thousand kilometres," said Rosina.

"It'll have been round the clock," Wang replied, running his finger round the wheel-arches. "Look at this rust!"
He stood up, and pressed down on the wing. The car gave
a loud creak. "It's a bit of a wreck. But still . . ."

Rosina nodded. She had always dreamt of owning a car,
though they weren't much use in Beijing, where traffic jams
were getting worse year by year. But for family outings to
the Great Wall or the Summer Palace . . . Imagine not
having to cram on to a coach, not having to be back at
Point 1 by Time 2; imagine being able to go wherever you
wanted, to find a quiet piece of countryside and pull out
the hamper and sit in the sun and—

Her husband had her by the hand and was leading her
away. She gave him a glance of resentment; he apologized.

"Someone was coming," he explained. "I didn't want
anyone to see us looking."

"Why not?"

"Because, er, it's rude." They walked a little further.
"Wu Weidong must have a top job, or be on the fiddle,"
Wang said suddenly.

"It's certainly something, owning a car. You know, you
ought to try and get hold of the Work Unit one more often.
At weekends, for example . . ."

They reached North Square—their destination, as Nanping Village Industries were hosting the Memorial Banquet.
Old Pigtail Mao was sitting on the old millstone, just as he
had been when Wang and Rosina first arrived in the village.

This time he didn't hobble away but fixed Wang with a stare.

"So you're Wang Anzhuang, then?" he said.

"Yes."

The old man grinned. He had one tooth. "I thought you were a ghost!"

Wang tried to look superior to this superstitious rustic. "Why?"

"Nobody told me you were coming back. I thought it was your father. Come to sort out that brother of yours." The old man mimed raising a glass to his lips.

"No," Wang said sadly.

"They're coming back, though, the ghosts," Old Mao went on. "Secretary Wu will be next."

A murder victim traditionally returns to haunt his or her killer. "Who will he be after?" Wang asked.

"Ha! That's your job to find out, isn't it, Inspector!"

"No. You have a police station here."

The old fellow tapped his head. "Fate has sent you, to keep the ghosts away," he said. Then he turned and began filling a long-stemmed clay pipe with tobacco.

Wu Weidong wandered round the tables, accepting condolences from the guests and thanking them for coming. The woman in the short dress followed him, looking vaguely bored. When he reached Wang's table, the inspector stood up and introduced himself.

"Wang Anzhuang, from Beijing. And this is my wife, Lin Xiangyu. My father was a close colleague of your father."

"Yes . . ." said Wu Weidong. "I remember him. Old Uncle Wang."

"That's the fellow."

Wu Weidong smiled and moved on to Rosina. "Lin. . . ?"

"Xiangyu. I'm sorry about what happened. Your father was a popular man by all accounts."

Wu Weidong nodded.

"It's a terrible thing, losing a loved one," Rosina went

on, putting as much sympathy as possible into her voice. Wu Weidong simply nodded mechanically, and moved on to the next guest, Station Chief Huang.

"Hello, Weidong. A fine ceremony, if I may say so."

"Thank you . . ."

"Very good speeches. And a magnificent selection of wreaths. That shows how highly everyone round here regarded your father."

"Yes . . . I guess it does . . ." The young man paused, as if he wanted to say more but was having trouble finding the words—then his female companion grabbed his arm and hustled him on to someone else.

"What an appalling woman," said Rosina, once the couple were out of earshot, "dragging him round like that. And those clothes! Who does she think she is?"

Later that evening, the station chief cornered Wang. "Can we have a word?" he said.

"Yes. Anything wrong?"

"Wu Weidong's car."

"What's the matter with it?"

"You were investigating it on the way here. I saw you."

"So?"

"Don't. Our enquiries are proceeding well, and I don't want prominent local people upset."

"He's not local."

"As the Secretary's son, he counts as local. And he's clearly in a delicate state at the moment. You have no case against him—"

"He has to be a suspect."

"Your evidence is circumstantial."

"You said yourself that there was a small number of people who were likely to be visiting Secretary Wu late at night—"

"I have clear evidence of a robbery." The chief looked Wang in the eye. "I had hoped you would be some help to us in our operations. I've always believed that policemen should work together against criminals, not against each other."

Wang looked downcast: he believed the same.

"For your information," the chief went on, "I've talked to the night guard at Party HQ and to several late-night noodle vendors in the main street. Nobody saw a blue Toyota the evening of the murder."

"Ah. Good. I admit I'm glad—but leads have to be followed: crimes don't always work out as we'd like them to." Wang paused. "Tell me, how long has Wu Weidong had that car?"

"Several years."

"So he's a big noise in Jinan?"

"No. But there's more money in the city than out here. Now will you leave the poor man alone?"

Wang gave a sigh. "OK."

9

"Young Wang! Good morning!"

"Hello, Wheels. How's Beijing?"

"Dusty. How's the countryside?"

"Violent. I can't wait to get back to a nice quiet inner city." Wang told the story of Secretary Wu's murder, then added: "I wonder if you could do me a small favour."

Wheels laughed. "I knew you hadn't rung just to say hello. What is it?"

"I want to know about someone who lives in Jinan. Wu Weidong, his name is."

"Wu ... Weidong ..." The man at the other end of the line was an old colleague of Wang's, confined to a wheelchair by a drug trafficker's bullet back in 1985. He was now librarian at CID Headquarters, and had access to more information than anyone else Wang knew, partly due to his official position, partly due to his new-found skill with computers. Especially hacking.

"You can't ask the local force?" said Wheels.

"It's better this way," Wang replied evasively.

Wheels sighed. Wang rarely wasted his time, just took a lot more of it than his superiors liked. "I'll try. As usual. Tell me more about him."

Wang did so. "Thanks, Wheels," he concluded. "You know I'm always grateful."

"I can almost taste that bottle of *Maotai* you're going to buy me."

Wang and Rosina weren't sure they had a right to attend Secretary Wu's cremation, a quieter, more intimate affair than the Memorial Meeting—but Deputy Yao had insisted. They rode into Wentai in a Red Flag limousine and watched a simple wooden coffin vanish down a squeaking conveyor belt.

"He's gone to meet Marx," said the deputy.

Wang looked round, to see if anyone registered the irony of this comment—unintended, surely? Wu's daughter was in tears, but she had been on the verge of crying all morning. Wu Weidong looked as cold as he had the previous day.

When the ashes were ready, they were placed in an ornamental urn with a picture of a phoenix on it. The party then drove back to Nanping, parking at the end of the tarmacked road. The last part of the journey was uphill, and made on foot.

The group soon strung out into a line. Assistant Xia and the sexton, a small wrinkled man in a Mao suit who had been a Daoist priest before the Party did away with such things, led the way. Wang and Rosina followed, then Wu's daughter, still in tears. Station Chief Huang and the Yaos followed them, together with representatives of local Party organizations. Wu Weidong and his partner brought up the rear.

"Come on, Francine," he exhorted her. (Wang grimaced: he found this new fashionable assumption of Western names ugly and unpatriotic—except for "Rosina," of course, which had a lovely musical ring to it.)

"You didn't say we were going mountaineering!" Francine snapped back. High heels and a tight skirt weren't ideal for hill-walking.

Finally they reached the summit of Snake Hill. A glorious view spread out in all directions; north over Weipowan, southwards towards Wentai, east and west across dragon-back hilltops towards the Yellow Sea and Xi'an respectively. The road they had just taken, wriggling off into the late-summer haze, seemed to be waving a farewell to the man who had fought so hard for its improvement. Wang had to admit this was a beautiful spot to rest. Good *feng-shui*, too, facing south and with water nearby.

The sexton began to scrape at the rocky earth with his spade. When a small hole had been dug, Wu Weidong placed the casket in it. Everyone went to collect a rock—there were plenty—to set around it: a small cairn soon built up. Weidong found a long flat stone to put over the top, then produced a wodge of paper from his pocket.

"Feudal superstition!" Mrs. Yao tutted in a stage whisper.

Wu Weidong bent down and placed the wodge in front of the cairn: his parting gift to his father. Secretary Wu would need these on his journey to the next world—the banknotes drawn on the Bank of Hell, the depictions of goods and provisions, the replica Party card. The sexton just happened to remember a Daoist prayer and to begin chanting it; the Secretary's son struck a match and set light to the papers; the flames leapt up and consumed the offerings in an instant, thus presenting them to the ghostly authorities waiting to receive Party Secretary Wu Changyan. A plume of smoke drifted out from the hillside, west towards the ancient heart of China.

Wu Weidong watched it impassively then began to cry.

"So he did care, after all," said Rosina.

"Possibly."

"Cynic."

"I'm a policeman. I've seen people fake all sorts of emotions."

"He looked genuine to me . . ."

They were sitting on the verandah of the guesthouse, looking up at the hill where Secretary Wu's ashes now lay, and drinking plum cordial, an old favourite drink of Wang's that Rosina was slowly getting to like too.

"I'd be more interested in that Francine woman if I were investigating the case," Rosina went on. "She didn't have a ring, and someone like that would have a ring if she were properly married—a big gold one with a huge fake jewel in it. How's this for a scenario? She catches herself a nice Party Secretary's son. He's besotted; he asks her to marry him. Then Father steps in, saying no. So he has to be got out of the way."

"Plenty of people marry without parental permission nowadays," Wang replied sharply.

Rosina glared at him, then fell silent. Mrs. Ming appeared and announced that dinner was ready.

"I've upset you, haven't I?" said Wang, picking another slice of cold salted duck.

"Yes. I thought that was a perfectly sensible suggestion I made about Wu Weidong's partner. You made it sound stupid."

"I'm sorry. It wasn't stupid. But I don't see how she could have got to the house."

"She's got legs. As she's keen to show everybody."

"She'd need transport. And it doesn't really account for the Secretary's mood just before the killing, either. Not if Wu didn't like her."

"Maybe he'd discovered some way of getting at her, and was looking forward to trying it out . . . Anyway, people get moods for all sorts of reasons. They're not exactly hard evidence, are they?"

"No," Wang replied quietly. "I've said I'm sorry."

"OK." Rosina stared at him for a long, long time. She wasn't sure how deeply he meant it, but was unwilling to push the point. They finished the starters in silence.

"I feel bad about getting involved in this," Wang said suddenly. "I made you a promise: this is a holiday. But the local police decided what had happened before they even got to the crime scene. The most likely conclusion is that a petty crook will get a bullet in the neck, and a murderer will go unpunished."

Rosina smiled. "D'you think I haven't realized that, from all the things you've told me?"

"No, but—"

"I want to be involved, that's all."

Wang looked uneasy. "This is a murder investigation."

"I've seen a hell of a lot more dead bodies than you have!"

His uneasiness grew. "That's not the point. I wouldn't walk into the Peace Hospital and start sticking needles into your patients."

"I wouldn't walk into Qianmen East Street and start issuing arrest warrants . . ." Rosina paused. "But we're not in Beijing, we're in the countryside. We've got a problem to solve. Together."

"Together?"

"I don't expect to be Dr. Watson," Rosina went on (like her husband, and many other Chinese, she knew the Holmes stories well: whenever she heard London mentioned, she saw a fogbound megalopolis teeming with horse-drawn carriages, ragged street-children and Capitalists in top hats). "I do expect to be listened to."

Wang nodded his head. "You're right," he said. "I was being arrogant. I'm sorry."

"Apology accepted," said Rosina, who then burst into tears.

She had hardly dried her eyes when Mrs. Ming came in and cleared away the starter plates with her usual clatter. When everything was on its tray, ready to leave, she took it up and headed for the door. Then she paused, and turned round again.

"You're a detective, aren't you, Mr. Wang?" she said.

"That's right."

She grinned, embarrassed. "I've been trying to get in touch with the local police for the last two days, but I just get a very stupid constable who says the station chief will call back. Then nobody does. I'm wondering—if you can help at all. You see, I'm getting worried about Mr. Lian."

"Lian?"

"Your fellow guest. I haven't seen him for several days."

"He seems to like his privacy."

"Yes, but he always said when he was going to miss his meals. I cooked him a lovely fish on Wednesday, and he never ate it. And since then . . ."

Wednesday was the day Secretary Wu had been murdered. "No sign of him?" said Wang.

"No. It sounds silly, but I'm worried someone may have killed him."

"Why would anyone want to do that?"

"Don't know. But I don't know why anyone would want to kill Secretary Wu." The manageress glanced nervously round the room. "They have them in the West, you know. Maniacs who go round murdering people for no reason."

"They have all sorts of unpleasant things in the West," the inspector replied. "This is China." But he picked up a chopstick and began spinning it in his fingers—a sure sign that his attention had been engaged. "Do you have any idea what Mr. Lian was doing here?"

"No."

"How did he fill his days?"

"Don't know. He used to walk a lot: he'd leave a pair of muddy boots outside his door every evening to be cleaned."

"What sort of mud?"

"All kinds."

"Was he the guest here of the local Party?"

"No. The order came from Jinan. Deputy Yao just put a rubber stamp on it."

"Yao? Not Wu?"

"The Secretary was usually too busy to do routine work like that."

"Shame. I'd like to see the order sometime, if that's possible."

Mrs. Ming suddenly looked embarrassed. Wang decided not to press her for the moment: papers can easily get lost, especially if they don't seem important. "Did Mr. Lian receive any visitors?"

"No."

"Nobody called for him, or wrote, or left any kind of message?"

"There was a letter that morning. Wednesday, I mean."

"Ah. What kind? Official? Private?"

"The address was handwritten."

"Can you tell me anything about the characters?"

Mrs. Ming paused. "A woman's hand, I'd say. Youngish." She smiled. "I've seen a lot of people filling in forms over the years."

"Excellent. Did you see the postmark?"

"No. It was inland mail, though, I'm sure."

"And Mr. Lian made no comment on it to you?"

"No."

"Shame . . . I'll see if there's anything I can do. In the meantime, keep trying the local police. I'll mention it to Station Chief Huang if I see him."

"That's very kind," said Mrs. Ming.

The lock opened easily. Wang and Rosina tiptoed into the room and flashed torches round it.

"Tidy fellow, wasn't he?" Rosina whispered.

The letter was the obvious thing to look for; the desk—the room was a mirror image of theirs—was the obvious place to look for it. The desk was locked. Try somewhere else before getting the picks out. The bin? Empty. The bedside table. No, though there was a book on it: *The Battle for Jinan*. In the book? No. In the bedside drawer? No. Try the wardrobe. All pockets of everything . . .

"Nice stuff," Wang commented.

"A bit old-fashioned," Rosina replied loftily. Tailormade Mao jackets, trousers in drab colours, a Western suit.

So it had to be the desk. The pick made short work of its lock: it was either not expected that visitors to the Government Guesthouse would be spied on, or intended that this should be easy.

Inside were more books. *A History of the Shandong Campaigns, 1945–9. Revolutionary Memoirs.* They were well thumbed and annotated: clearly Lian was a lover of

Revolutionary history. Was the letter in any of these? No. Wang pulled open the desk drawers one by one, but they were all empty. He even checked the space behind the drawers: nothing.

"Better check out the bathroom," he said.

"For a letter?"

"You can learn a lot about someone from their bathroom. You keep hunting around here."

Rosina frowned but did as she was asked; Wang went into the bathroom. Check the obvious things: toothbrush, razor, soap, towel-flannel. These were all present, so Mr. Lian had either gone out intending to return or had left in a hurry. The cabinet produced a bottle of Tiger Balm, half a box of Deer Brand Virility Tablets and a bottle of "101" Hair Restorer. None of the telltale medicines that sudden deaths often left behind them. What about—

"Anzhuang!"

Rosina's voice sounded urgent: Wang's immediate thought was that Mr. Lian had chosen this minute to reappear. He began concocting a face-saving story.

"Come and look!" Rosina went on.

Wang went back into the main room. Rosina was holding open one of Lian's books at a well-thumbed page.

"Read this!"

He did so.

". . . Our forces suffered a small setback when a column of a hundred guerillas from Yan'an and seven local guides was ambushed in Snake Valley, near Nanping. Forty-two guerillas and three guides were killed.

"The Guomindang had shown no interest in Snake Valley until that fateful evening; they took no interest in it afterwards. Their troops were carefully stationed; there is no possibility that they just stumbled on the Communist forces. The question is how the enemy knew the column was going to be there. Either its progress was secretly observed, or someone who knew the plans betrayed them. The former possibility, while it cannot be discounted, is unlikely: commanders took great care to conceal their movements. Regrettably, treachery remains the most likely explanation.''

"Now look at this." Rosina turned to the back of the book. On the endpaper, someone had scribbled a list of characters. Names. One of them was Wu Changyan.

"That's Secretary Wu's name, isn't it?" said Rosina.

Wang nodded.

"Could it be a coincidence?" she went on—though she knew what Wang would say.

10

The inspector phoned Beijing next morning.

"You're in a hurry," said Wheels.

"Yes. Er, I need some more information. On a second suspect."

A laugh came back down the line. "I suppose this Wu Weidong doesn't matter any longer..."

"Have you got something on him already?"

"Oh yes, everything," the hacker replied, his voice full of sarcasm. "Who's this new guy?"

"He's called Lian. Lian Gang."

"Lian Gang. 'Forge Steel.' Sounds like one of those aliases that Party members took in the old days."

"Could be. He might well have been a partisan in 1947."

"That should narrow it down to several hundred thousand. I believe the Emei Shan do a very nice banquet for two. Courting couples, or people who owe friends for particularly big favours."

"The Snake Valley ambush..." said Acting Secretary Yao, shaking his head. "Now there was a terrible tragedy. Of course, I wasn't in Nanping at the time: I was in Manchuria under Lin Biao.'' He spoke the name of the great, but later disgraced, general with hesitant admiration. ''So I can't tell you much about it. Don't know who could, really.'' He stared out of the window. ''They got the traitor, of course. Your father was on some kind of enquiry board, back in the fifties . . .''

''D'you still have a transcript?'' said Wang eagerly.

''Don't know. Better ask young, er, what's his name. Fellow who looks after the filing . . .''

''When?'' said Assistant Xia.

''Sometime in the fifties, Acting Secretary Yao said.''

The young man shook his head. The fifties meant real memories to Wang: to Xia, they were like an ancient dynasty.

''We had a clear-out a year or so back. Secretary Wu went through anything pre-1976, kept a few things and said we could throw the rest away. We haven't got the space, you see.''

''I'd like to see what he kept,'' said Wang.

''No problem.''

A day of mole-like burrowing in the cellar of the main offices revealed nothing. ''The police might have something,'' Assistant Xia suggested.

''I've already heard from Mrs. Ming,'' said Station Chief Huang. ''I'm surprised at your bringing the subject up. We've got a murder hunt on. One old man going for a long walk is hardly relevant. And what was this about files? Snake Valley ambush? No, we haven't got anything on that. Why should we? Try Party HQ. Old Yao will know about it if anyone does.''

There was one bus a day into Wentai town, then a choice of several to Jinan, the state capital. All of the latter were equally uncomfortable.

''I'd rather ride that jeep,'' said Rosina, as they went over another bump. A Western backpacker, who had got the seat over the rear wheel, shot up into the air and hit his head on the metal roof.

"I tried," Wang replied. "It wasn't available."

Rosina scowled. Whole families had crammed on to the unpadded double seats; the aisle was blocked with straphangers. The man standing beside Rosina kept digging the corner of a wicker basket into the side of her head, perhaps as a hint that she should budge up and let him sit down. He was out of luck.

They pulled into a village, and the bus was immediately surrounded by vendors—especially the window space occupied by the foreigner. One man was offering him a bottle of iced tea at an outrageous price: the big-nose leaned out of the window to bargain and was sick. The vendor, on whom most of the vomit landed, began screaming insults; everyone else roared with laughter. Rosina passed a plastic water-bottle back to the ailing visitor.

He muttered something that sounded vaguely like *xiexie* (thank you); Rosina gave him a maternal smile, at the same time wondering what on earth possessed people from rich Western countries to travel in this way. And hoping that she wasn't going to conclude the journey by sharing his fate.

Rosina tottered up the steps of Party HQ, Jinan. Wang handed her an identity card. "You'll need this," he said.

She began to delve in her bag. "I've got mine already."

"Use this one."

Rosina glanced at it. "It's false!"

"Of course."

"Why?" she hissed.

"I'm not having Beijing find out I've been doing detective work on my holiday."

"But couldn't we get into trouble?"

"Possibly."

"You're doing this deliberately."

"Memorize your name. Li Mitian."

A guard at the door, with a Type 56 Kalashnikov copy, asked to see their cards. Wang handed his over; the guard glanced at it and gave it back. Rosina did the same: he looked at her face, then at the photo, then at her face . . .

"I know—she has beautiful eyes," said Wang. The guard laughed and let them in.

A receptionist was sitting behind a desk, under a large five-pointed star and a photograph of Premier Deng Xiaoping on his visit to Shenzhen in 1992.

"Guo Lingyang, Public Security, Chengdu," said Wang, in a Sichuanese accent Rosina couldn't hope to mimic. "I need access to files in your library. Here's my accreditation."

He handed over his card. The receptionist stared at it, then picked up the phone. "I'll need to check," he said.

"Is that really necessary?"

"Yes."

Rosina tried to guess how far it was to the door. Not that that mattered—they'd also have to run beyond the range of that Kalashnikov.

"Lingyang. Guo Lingyang . . ." the receptionist was saying. "He is? Fine." He put the phone down. "Your colleague's name?"

"Li Mitian," said Rosina, flashing a smile at the old man.

He didn't smile back but he didn't phone anyone, either. Or question her accent. "Down the big corridor, through the doors on the left at the end. You'll see a sign."

"Thank you."

"We have a little arrangement with Chengdu," Wang explained once they were out of earshot. "Every now and then, I get a call just to check we have a Guo Lingyang at our office. Usually the caller has a Sichuanese accent."

"Bloody clever," said Rosina.

"I still don't see why Chengdu is interested in Nanping," said the librarian, treating Wang and Rosina to a suspicious stare.

"That's Chengdu's business," Wang replied coldly. He handed back the printout she had given him, of files relating to Nanping village. "I'd like the asterisked one, please."

"That'll be ten yuan. We have to charge nowadays."

Wang gave her a ten-yuan note, one of the new ones with Mao, Zhou Enlai and Liu Shaoqi on, then he and Rosina sat down on blue plastic chairs with legs of unequal length and grinned at each other. The librarian eventually reappeared with a small manilla envelope. Wang took it with all the reserve he could muster, then crossed to a plastic table where he and his silent companion opened it.

RECORDS OF OFFICIAL ENQUIRY

DATE:	June 5th, 6th, 7th 1952
LOCATION:	Party HQ, Jinan
SUBJECT:	Ambush at Snake Valley
LEADER:	Comrade Hu Fenglao
TEAM MEMBERS:	Comrade Shi Yibing (People's Liberation Army, 34th Division), Comrade Bo Rui (Cadre, Jinan Party), Comrade Wang Jingfu (Secretary, Nanping Branch).

Wang and Rosina read together. An introductory address by Comrade Hu on the importance of unmasking traitors at this time of national emergency. Expressions—the report was verbatim—of support from the committee. Including Comrade Wang Jingfu.

My father's words, Wang thought.

Members of the ambushed force then presented themselves before the committee and were given an initial cross-questioning. Comrade Hu had an aggressive style, bordering on the accusatory, but nobody admitted anything significant.

Written submissions followed, from other partisans now unable to attend. All of these expressed shock at the ambush; no one had expected anything or had any idea as to how it had come about. Then the local guides took the floor: four of them, the four names Lian had scribbled in his book.

"D'you know who any of the others are?" Rosina whispered.

"No."

Wu had been the last to be questioned. Wang did a quick sum: the tetchy old man Wang had faced in his villa would then have been a lad of about twenty. He tried to imagine what the Secretary would have looked like, standing there, before Wang's own father—and how Wu would have felt. Wang still found his own interview with Secretary Wu puzzling—why had his host overreacted to his and Rosina's contact with the Fei family? Maybe this was the reason . . .

"I agree that treachery is the most likely cause of the tragedy," Wu had told the enquiry. "But I am unable to suggest who might be responsible. My comrades from Nanping are of excellent character, and it would be disgraceful even to suspect the fighters from Yan'an who helped us liberate our province. For myself I can only swear my innocence."

"This is not as full or frank an answer as I had hoped," had been Comrade Hu's reply.

"I cannot implicate anyone. I have no information."

"A true lover of the Party seeks out its enemies with unceasing energy, Comrade Wu."

Next day, the tribunal had asked specific individuals to submit to questioning in greater detail—particularly about their past. One man called Shen Zirong had been forced to admit to a particularly poor personal history. He had absented himself from duty on several occasions. He was known to have relatives who supported the Guomindang. He had once been heard to question the authority of Chairman Mao and Comrade Kang Sheng . . .

Wang read this part of the transcript with gathering unease. His father played no role in the questioning, but he was still partially responsible. Shen Zirong was being set up as a scapegoat.

Shen had known this too. Suddenly the man was on his

knees, "a most unsoldierly position," begging the commission to believe his innocence.

"Ask Sergeant Han," Shen Zirong had said. "He knows I'm innocent."

"Sergeant Han Haotong is not present."

"Ask him. Somehow. I beg you!"

"Sergeant Han is currently fighting American and British imperialist forces in Korea. It has not been possible to contact him."

"You must do so, in order to be fair."

"The Party decides what is and what isn't fair."

Shen Zirong had been placed under arrest.

Proceedings on the third day were brief. It was announced that under questioning from the Public Security Bureau, Shen Zirong had confessed his crimes. He had been for many years a Guomindang agent. He had been guilty of acts of political sabotage—including sowing dissent among Party ranks. He had been taken out that morning and shot.

Wang sat for a long time with his head in his hands. Finally Rosina put an arm round him, earning a glare from the librarian.

"My father . . ." Wang whispered to her. "He was involved in that. The murder of an innocent man."

"It was a long time ago."

"He would have put his signature on Shen Zirong's death warrant."

"What else could he have done?"

"He always told me to do what was right. 'Be prepared to die for justice.' "

"He had to survive. He had to look after his family. Just as you did, in the Cultural Revolution."

"Yes . . ." said Wang. He was silent for a moment, then slammed the table with his fist.

"Ssh," said Rosina.

Wang gritted his teeth. He knew she was right. He shut the file as gently as he could, dried the mark of a terrible, unmanly tear from his eyes, took ten deep *qigong* breaths, then took the file back.

"Do you keep records of who's taken files out, and when?" he asked in what was left of his Sichuanese accent.

"Not 'who,' unless it's out at the moment. As for 'when,' there should be a stamp on the docket." She checked. "Yes, it was consulted last week."

"And before that?"

"Nothing. What's happening?"

"Security matter," said Wang.

The librarian took the envelope back without so much as a glance at it.

"One last thing," said Wang, pulling a piece of paper out of his pocket. "Can you tell me whose signature this is?"

The librarian stared at the scrawled characters and shook her head. "That's Director Yi's. He died last year."

Wang and Rosina walked up through Nanping from the bus station (a patch of mud with a tin hut on it). Rosina had a bag under her arm: after their visit to Party HQ, they'd done some sightseeing and rather more shopping.

"So Lian forged a signature to get his room at the guest-house," she said, with just a little too much eagerness in her voice. "What a crook!"

"He probably did it for security reasons," Wang replied.

"He liked playing games?"

"He meant it. If he was a cadre in the Mao years, he'll probably be obsessed with secrecy. And if he suspected the local Party Secretary of treachery . . ."

"How did he know Mrs. Ming wouldn't check?"

"I don't know. But she didn't, did she? And I'm sure he'd have had some story ready if she had done." He fell silent.

They stopped at a late-night food stall, and sucked their way through bowls of noodles in delicious spicy gravy. The vendor's tureen made a bubbling sound, her hurricane lamp hissed, a radio played somewhere, a bicycle went by jangling its bell: Rosina heard all these sounds with great acuteness, as you do when you want to hear something else.

"That business with the execution of Shen Zirong . . ."

said Wang. "I still can't believe my father would have connived at that . . ." His voice tailed away.

Rosina took his hand. "Let's get out of here. We can go to Qingdao, book into a cheap hotel, get a bit of time on a beach. I'm sure Old Yao will sign all the papers we need."

"We can't leave things as they are." He looked Rosina in the eye. "Can we?"

"No," she replied.

11

Wang and Rosina spent the next day walking. By the evening they both felt tired but in much better spirits. Late summer can be one of the best times of year in Shandong, and the weather had been in a generous mood all day. They took their dinner on the verandah, watching the sun set over the village; they drank some more of Wang's cordial and felt happy to be together and untroubled. When the phone in their room began ringing, neither wanted to answer it—but it was persistent, and eventually Wang gave up.

"What are you up to?" asked Wheels Chai.

"Sitting with my wife watching the sunset," Wang replied.

"How nice. Now, I've got some stuff for you. D'you want to hear it, or shall I just sing you a love song?"

"Tell me what you've found out."

"Right. Wu Weidong works for the state government in Jinan. As a clerk in the maintenance department. A pretty junior one: he earns about four hundred yuan a month. You know how far that goes nowadays. But—get this!—he drives a car. A Toyota. He's had it since 1988. Also, he and his partner—they're not married, by the way—moved to a new apartment in June, in one of the smartest parts of

town. Wu Weidong took out a huge loan with the Shandong
Industry Bank to pay for it.''

"Ah . . .''

"His partner's name is Lei Luren. She works in a hair-
dressing salon. One of these private places where business-
men's wives spend more than we earn in a month. But the
profits go to the management: Lei just gets a salary. So
you've got two people, living like senior Party officials on
next to nothing. Neither has a criminal record, by the way.''

"I see . . .''

"Thought you'd be interested.''

"Yes. Thanks. Any luck on Lian Gang? He's disap-
peared, you see . . .''

"So far, he could be one of two hundred and fifty-three
people. But there are plenty of other places to check. None
of my two hundred and fifty-three Lian Gangs are on record
as having participated in the Shandong campaign, so maybe
that's just as well. You want me to keep looking?''

"Please.'' Wang paused. "Look, while you're on that—''

"Not another suspect!''

"Not exactly. But I need to trace a fellow called Han.
Han Haotong. He was a sergeant in the PLA and fought in
Korea. All I want is a current address.''

"All? You know what military records are like.''

"I know how good you are at this.''

Wang heard a curse. Then the sound of a police-issue
biro scratching on paper. "Han . . . Haotong . . . I think
we'd better have champagne with that dinner.''

"You find me Sergeant Han, and I'll keep the stuff flow-
ing all evening.'' Wang knew how much his friend loved
the sparkling drink from former Soviet Georgia.

"Who was that?'' Rosina asked, when Wang came back
from the call.

Wang told her.

"And what did he say?''

Wang told her.

"I think we should go for another walk,'' he added.

"Where?''

"To where Secretary Wu used to live. Wu Weidong and your friend Francine are staying there while they sort the old man's effects out."

Wang thought for a moment about what Station Chief Huang would have to say about such an action. But only a moment.

They met the station chief about halfway to their destination. He, Constable Kong and a man Wang didn't know, probably on loan from the Wentai force, were standing on the main road across the pass, smoking cigarettes and looking bored. Huang had a clipboard. Wang guessed what they were doing, but asked anyway.

"Stopping any passers-by," the chief replied, "and asking them if they were here this time last week—the night of the murder."

Wang cursed inwardly. "Any luck?"

"Not yet."

"I'd be interested to know if you *do* find anything."

The chief looked at him closely.

"One of the many areas of potential cooperation . . ." Wang added.

"I shall be in my office from ten till half past tomorrow morning."

Wang and Rosina began to move off.

"Don't go bothering Wu Weidong and his wife," Huang called out.

"We wouldn't dream of it," Wang replied.

There were lights on in the villa.

"D'you think we should?" Rosina whispered.

Wang put his finger to his lips. "Follow me."

There was a breach in the garden wall, and beyond that, a clump of bushes from which there was a side-on view of the living room. A poor view, but the best one available: the Secretary's office might have been easy to spy on from outside; his living room was not. Wang and Rosina crawled through the wall and took up position behind the bushes.

"It's damp . . ." said Rosina.

"Patience and tolerance of discomfort are essential on a stake-out," Wang replied, then took her hand.

Wu Weidong and Francine were watching TV. The sudden changes of brightness made it appear as if a tiny electrical storm were raging in the room. A familiar, jingling tune announced advertisements.

"Not saying much, are they?" said Rosina, as the programme resumed. "I think they've had a row. They're sitting apart; they look locked in their own thoughts."

Wang nodded. Wu Weidong looked particularly preoccupied. About what? Francine lit a cigarette. Nobody said anything. Time passed.

"It's very damp," Rosina whispered.

More adverts—they seemed to be getting longer and more frequent. Wang longed for the days when you had a couple of ads for Five Flowers umbrellas, Gold Lion shirts ("A world for men!") or Lux soap every half hour or so, and the rest of the time actually saw what you had tuned in to watch.

Francine lit another cigarette.

"D'you have to?" Weidong snapped.

"There's not a lot else to do here, is there?"

"Don't go on like that again. We've started this, and we have to finish it."

"You spent a long time in the vicinity of Wu Weidong's house last night," said Station Chief Huang. "That road goes nowhere."

"There's a path at the end that leads up to a view point," Wang explained. "It's a nice place to sit and look at the stars."

The chief scowled. City life certainly rotted people. "Here's the list you asked for. The people I stopped, and what they had to say."

Wang glanced down it. Two men, a little drunk according to the notes, heading over the pass. A shoe-repair man coming the other way. Two grain merchants . . .

"The merchants are the only ones who admitted to using the road the previous week," said the chief, pre-empting

Wang's question. "They play bridge with a friend who has
a villa up there."

Wang nodded. Since Deng Xiaoping had taken up
bridge, the game had become fashionable among the
wealthy.

"They fit the description of Driver Gao's two men," the
chief went on. "They can be eliminated from the investigation."

"Did they see anyone the night of the murder?"

"Only Zhang Hong."

"Who's Zhang Hong?"

"The local schoolteacher. One of the witnesses has a
child at the school; Zhang wished him good evening as he
passed; they had a brief conversation."

"That's interesting."

Huang scowled. "Teacher Zhang is highly respected
here." Noticing the look of disapproval on Wang's face,
he added: "It's hardly the action of a killer, going round
saying good evening to people on your way to a murder.
Or do they do that in Beijing?"

"You're assuming that the murder was premeditated."

"Hmph. We'll be bringing him in for an interview, anyway."

"What time did the witnesses see this teacher?"

"About eight o'clock."

Wang nodded. "He has to be a suspect. He was a bit
early for his appointment, that's all. So he waited around
while Secretary Wu and I were, er, having our discussion,
then came in . . ."

"Teacher Zhang isn't a murderer."

"Tell me more about him."

"He was born here, then went away to study in Jinan.
Then he came back here to teach, which makes us very
lucky to have him. As you know, once people go to the
cities, they usually stay there." The chief gave Wang a
glance of obvious disapproval. "He's been at the school
for eight years now. He does an excellent job—despite certain, well, ideological lapses."

"Liberal, is he?"

"Oh, no. Old-fashioned Maoist. Like his uncle."

"His uncle?"

"The Red Tiger. The man who led all those Red-Guard raids back in the late sixties. The man who—"

"Zhang!" said Wang. "I wonder . . . Do you have any objection if I go and talk to him?"

"Yes. He should have an official interview first."

"This will be purely about old times. His uncle would have known my father."

Station Chief Huang looked at his guest. Was he lying? Did it matter?

"I shall make no mention of the murder," Wang went on.

"You suspect him, don't you?"

"A promise is a promise."

The chief frowned. To think he'd welcomed this man when he arrived in the village. Now here the bastard was, meddling, upsetting prominent local people who could affect his own position in the Party . . .

"Two sets of eyes can often be better than one," Wang went on. "Cooperation, you said. And if you're convinced he's not a killer, what harm can it do? I just want to meet him, that's all."

Huang sighed. "No accusations. And no questions about last Wednesday night. OK?"

"OK."

Teacher Zhang lived in a courtyard on the outskirts of the town. The step was scrubbed; the door had a well-oiled mechanical bell-push; when Wang rang, somebody answered at once—a little girl in dungarees, a T-shirt and a big red bow in her hair. She showed Wang into the main yard, where vegetables grew in neat rows.

"Can I help you?" Teacher Zhang was a man in his late thirties, balding but tall and healthy looking.

Wang introduced himself, adding: "You probably know my brother."

"Yes . . ." Zhang replied cautiously. "You'd better come in."

The inspector followed him through a large patio window into a spacious living room—the Zhangs had clearly been able to keep their courtyard to themselves.

"Sit down," said Zhang, pointing to a sofa with two perfectly aligned cushions on it. "I hope you're enjoying your return to Nanping. People still speak very highly of your father here."

"Thank you."

"Many people wish he were still our Party Secretary. Can I get you some tea?"

"Yes . . ."

"I know, the local stuff is undrinkable. A typical produce of so-called private enterprise—fob the buyer off with the worst possible quality goods. I have some Dragon Well here. Chairman Mao's favourite."

"That would be very welcome."

While the teacher was away making the tea, Wang looked round the walls of the room. Photographs, including several of Mao. Books, mostly from the Mao era, plus a few modern neo-Marxists like He Xin. Certificates, from the Young Pioneers and Teacher Training College in Jinan; the last one dated 1985. Most came from an earlier era, and praised Zhang's parents, aunt and uncle for participation in (the later ones said "leadership of") voluntary communal projects.

Wang smiled. He still admired the spirit behind these certificates. Selflessness, hard work, loyalty . . . Then a picture of Xu Yifeng came into his mind. The Red Tiger had sent her to freeze to death in a labour camp.

Zhang was back with the tea. "What brings you here?" he asked, still without warmth.

"The past," Wang replied.

Teacher Zhang sighed. "I didn't really know your father. I wish I had."

"He was a colleague of your uncle, though, wasn't he?"

"They fought side by side in the Revolution!"

"They're old comrades, then," Wang said, trying to lighten the mood. "Old comrades that are now being forgotten: that memorial in Snake Valley seems to be in a terrible state."

Zhang broke into a smile. "How good to hear someone say that! I've been trying to get something done about that memorial for ages, but nobody will listen. There seems to be an official policy of forgetting all about it." The teacher shook his head. "Of course, now they're going to flood the thing, I guess it doesn't matter so much. But I think they ought to build a new one, further up the hillside . . . You know how much money they were planning to spend on those dams, don't you?"

Wang didn't want to appear too nosy, and lied.

"Over a million yuan," said Zhang. "A million yuan. Think of the debt that would create for us in the village. And profit, for those moneylenders. It makes me sick." He scowled. "The farm should be a communal project. My mother visited the Red Flag Canal at Dazhai. She said there was pride on the faces of the people there like she had never seen anywhere. Why? Because they built it with their own hands." The teacher looked his visitor in the eye. "That's all gone, now—any joy in belonging to something bigger than oneself, any sense of duty or community. Money's all that matters. If you've got money, you can do anything. You can flood a valley, wash away memories, grab land rights—*aiya*, I hate those people." He grimaced; the hate was real and deep. "But what can ordinary working people do?"

"Protest? There's a group, isn't there?"

"Huh! They're a bunch of reactionary hypocrites. Most of them own land under threat; all they want to do is argue up the price. It's just like that business back in "eighty-nine: people using Western-style 'liberal' slogans to cover up self-interest." He paused, realizing he hadn't sounded out his visitor's views on Tiananmen. Wang replied with a grave, meaningless nod, the kind of gesture people normally interpreted as they wished.

Zhang appeared reassured. "Refill for your tea, Inspector?"

"Thanks."

While the teacher went to fetch the Thermos, Wang took another look round the room. The child, who was now playing hopscotch in the garden, had made little impression on the place, except for a box of toys in one corner and a collection of comics on the bookshelf (way out of her reach: clearly she was rationed).

"That memorial," he said, when Zhang got back. "You're telling me that nobody even mentions it nowadays?"

"Nobody."

"Or the ambush?"

"No."

"I guess people want to forget. Did they ever find out who betrayed the column?"

"I think so," the teacher replied. "Wasn't somebody shot for it, back in the fifties?"

"I don't recall." Wang grinned. "Does the name Lian Gang mean anything to you?"

Zhang's puzzlement appeared genuine. "I'm afraid not. It's a nice old Party alias, though. 'Forge steel.' I don't know what people are calling themselves nowadays. 'Make money?' 'Line pocket?' 'Accept bribe?' " He laughed. "Who is this fellow?"

"Just an old comrade of my father. And of your uncle, too. I was wondering if you knew anything about him."

"No."

"Shame. Old comrades seem to be a dying breed!"

The teacher nodded, then glanced up for a moment with a look of horror. Wang kept an affable smile on his face, as if he hadn't noticed, and Zhang relaxed at once. The inspector took another sip of tea. Chairman Mao's favourite.

12

Wang sat on the verandah, drinking afternoon tea and filling in a notebook. A page for each suspect. A page for each of the slash-marks across the apparently placid face of Nanping village.

Mr. Lian. What had been in that letter? Information about the Snake Pass traitor? To the effect that the traitor was Secretary Wu? Maybe Lian had gone to confront the traitor, taken revenge, then fled, overcome with revulsion at what he'd done. Maybe—but where was the proof? Come on, Wheels, find me Sergeant Han!

Wu Weidong. What was it he had started and had to finish? A plan to kill his father and pay off his debts? The trouble was that Wang couldn't see what Wu Weidong's plan had been. His father had no money. Except, Wang thought, those paintings. But even in a city, they would be difficult to sell: Wu Weidong would need help in realizing anything like their true value, and that help would cost him dear. What would pay off his debt at a stroke was the kick-back that people like Anming and Fei Baoren claimed his father to have been after. But that made the Secretary more use to his son alive than dead, surely . . .

Francine. Maybe Rosina was right. Wu Weidong would

know his father's financial situation; Francine might not. She might have thought the old man was rich, and that on his death Wu Weidong would become rich too. But there was no guarantee that would make *her* rich. Wang frowned, then wrote "Establish alibi" against her name.

Teacher Zhang. Wang thought of the teacher's expression when he had made that comment about old campaigners being a "dying breed." And the teacher had been seen in the area around the time of the murder. He clearly disliked the reforming Secretary Wu—but enough to kill him?

Then there was the hate-mail. And, of course, the official theory, of a bungled raid. Could Station Chief Huang be right, after all?

"No!" Wang said aloud, with a vehemence that surprised even him.

"What's up? Are you all right?" Rosina had been in the room, talking on the phone, but was now right behind him.

"Yes. Fine."

She put a hand on his shoulder. "I've something to ask you."

"What?"

"Baoren wants me to go to another meeting of her group."

"You should go."

"Even after this fuss with Secretary Wu?"

"He's dead. His successor hasn't said anything about the group. So go." Wang paused. "Is Baoren's father going to be there?"

"I'm not afraid of him."

"That's fine, then." Wang paused. "What time is the meeting?"

"Six."

The inspector glanced at his watch. "I'd like to come too."

The meeting was held in an old barn. The first person they met on arrival was Baoren, who insisted on joining them.

"My father isn't well enough to attend," she explained.

They went in and found a bench in an unlit corner: Wang

wanted to watch, not be watched. The room filled up, mainly with peasant farmers. Then Manager Wei entered. To Wang's surprise, the businessman walked out in front of the audience and called the meeting to order.

"Since we last met, Secretary Wu has, er, passed on—"

"Good thing too!" shouted someone.

Manager Wei looked unmoved. "This clearly has implications for our cause. Until a new Secretary is appointed, it is unlikely any progress will be made with the fish-farm—"

"What about Yao?" someone asked.

"That old shrivelled dick," muttered someone else.

"When the appointment is made, we must be in a position to put our case clearly and forcefully to them—"

"You'd never force anyone," said a voice.

"You've got plenty of money. This doesn't matter a fart to you," another shouted.

"You can see how angry people are," Baoren whispered. "I'm sorry if they're not very polite, but . . ."

Manager Wei began defending himself against a rising tide of criticism from the floor; a tide that rose in volume but deteriorated in quality. Wang looked round at the audience: he'd always felt proud of his rural roots, but this rabble . . . The meeting was degenerating into uproar. A man was on his feet, waving a piece of paper at the manager. Another was bellowing insults. A third—

Wang started with horror. And embarrassment.

"Wei Shaojia!" shouted Wang Anming, jumping on to a stool. "What have you done for us? It's just luck that old Wu died; we'll get a new boss and you'll be patting his arse in no time, too. We need a new chairman! And some action!"

This comment was greeted with loud cheers.

Don't do this, Anming.

"I propose Wang Anming take the job!" shouted a man in a green Mao jacket. "Let's take a vote on it. Our new chairman, Wang Anming! All in favour raise their hand."

You don't understand what you're getting into.

A copse of hands, a wood, a forest . . .

"*Stop!*" Only a woman's voice could carry across the din. It belonged to Fei Baoren, who was advancing into the light. "This is not the way to run things!"

The crowd fell silent.

"Manager Wei has influence," she went on. "He can argue our cause. What kind of action do you have in mind, Anming? Violence? Do you want to play straight into the hands of the Party?"

"I want my land!" said the man in the green jacket.

"Don't we all?"

The man fixed her with a glance of real hatred, looked about to let fly at her, then turned back to his audience. 'We need a new leader. Manager Wei has let us down. We've wasted too much time. I happen to know that contracts have been submitted. Maybe they've even been awarded. Meanwhile we've achieved nothing! I say—"

Anming walked up to him and put a hand on his shoulder. "Fei Baoren is right," he said slowly.

Green-jacket rounded on him. "You—"

"She's right," Anming repeated. "I got carried away. I offer my apologies to the chair."

"No!"

"Yes." Anming walked across to Manager Wei and shook his hand.

"Your apology is accepted," said Wei.

The audience fell silent. Even the man in the green jacket went and sat down, though the look on his face undoubtedly meant that the group hadn't heard the last of him.

"Thank you," Wang whispered to Baoren, now back in her seat.

Ten minutes later, the meeting closed. The crowd began to leave. Wang watched them go: only when the room was virtually empty did he get to his feet and emerge into the light.

"Wang Anzhuang!" said Manager Wei, who was gathering up papers. "I know your wife has an interest in our cause, but I didn't expect to see you here. I'm sorry it wasn't a more constructive meeting."

"I'm sorry my brother was part of the disruption."

"A very small part of it. People think I'm in the pocket of the local Party, just because I don't rant and rave."

"If it wasn't for Manager Wei, the group would have been disbanded by the police long ago," Baoren put in.

Wei didn't contradict that statement, merely finished gathering his papers. "Secretary Wu and I had very fundamental differences of opinion on many things. But he respected my views—as far as he respected anyone else's views. And he knew how important my business is to Nanping."

"How well did you know the Secretary?" Wang asked.

"As well as anyone outside his family."

"No . . . Perhaps we should talk about him sometime."

"Do so now, if you like. I must go back to my office to finish off some paperwork—come with me, and let me show you the factory. And your wife must come, too."

Baoren, uninvited, backed away. In an instant, she was rich-peasant category again. A perpetual, irredeemable outsider.

"Thanks for the invitation," said Rosina, "but Baoren and I have things to discuss."

"Thanks," said Baoren, once the two men had gone.

"That's all right. That bloody manager had no right to say that."

"He was only being polite to you."

"And what about you?"

"Old habits die hard."

"Too damn hard," Rosina muttered, then shook her head. 'Do you want to go to that tea house again? They're open till eight."

"Could do . . ." Baoren paused. "Come to my home. If you can put yourself on the line for me, I can do the same for you."

"But your father . . ."

"He'll have to like it. He's been a real burden recently. He thinks he's ill, even though the doctor says there's nothing wrong with him. Come on, Rosina."

They walked back to the old house, across the fields,

over a stream and up the stone-flagged path. Inside the
yard, Baoren insisted they entered the accommodation by
the main door and thus passed through the main room to
get to Baoren's bedsit. Fei Zhaoling was sitting in a chair,
reading a magazine. He glanced up at his new guest.

"Hello," said Rosina nervously.

The old man simply nodded his head, and went back to
reading.

"He doesn't look ill," said Rosina, once they were in
Baoren's room. "He's depressed about this fish-farm business, probably."

Baoren shrugged. "I've never felt this before, but part
of me wants to tell him to rot." She winced. "That's awful,
isn't it?"

"No. You've given up more than most people would for
him. A little anger isn't out of place."

Baoren smiled. "I guess not. It feels so disloyal. He's
done a lot for me, too. Did I tell you about the agent?"

"No."

"This man suddenly started courting me. Luckily he was
rather ugly and hadn't the first idea how to approach a
woman with any intelligence. But he was very persistent.
Then I found out he was from Public Security, and that
there'd been this plan to blackmail me, so I'd betray the
protest group. Father is a very gentle person, but when he
heard about this—he went round to the man's house and
punched him in the face. The authorities were so embarrassed, they ignored the incident." She smiled at the
thought of once having fought back at the Party. "You'll
want some tea, won't you?"

"Decent stuff . . ."

"Of course. Come through to the kitchen." Baoren's request necessitated another trip through the main room.
Again, Fei Zhaoling looked up at Rosina: this time he muttered something that might have been hello. Progress.

Manager Wei's workplace was not too different to the inspector's own: cramped, functional, overflowing with paper. The phones were more modern, with push-button dials

and various memory functions; a computer sat and stared blankly at them from a corner. The visitor's seat was more comfortable too.

"Fancy a beer?" said the manager, crossing to one of the cabinets that opened to reveal a fridge. "Chinese or import?"

Chinese, Wang thought patriotically to himself. "Import," he said. The two men opened their cans. Wei began to talk.

"Secretary Wu and I both wanted the same things for Nanping. So we were allies. But look at how allies fall out . . ." Wang didn't need to be reminded of the purges of Party faithfuls that littered the history of People's China. 'Wu didn't understand management," Wei continued. "Like Chairman Mao, he thought that if enough people struggle hard enough for something, they get it. But things don't happen like that nowadays. The fish-farm would have been a disaster. Even if it had worked as intended, with no environmental problems, cost overruns and so on, it would never have recouped the initial investment. It was far too grandiose a scheme."

"So why was Wu so keen to build it?"

"I've really no idea."

"None at all?"

"My guess is that he became overconfident. That happens a lot in business. People pull off a few good deals and start thinking they can do anything. Then they move out of their depth, and lose everything. The Secretary was a very stubborn man—just the sort to do that. He would have ended up bankrupting this village. D'you know how much it was going to cost to build those dams?"

"Yes," said Wang.

"Then you'll know what I mean."

"I don't understand finance. The figures looked large to me. Where would the money have come from?"

"Banks. No problem in getting the stuff. But keeping up the repayments . . . I think Secretary Wu thought central government would bail him out if things went wrong. But they don't do that sort of thing any longer."

"Would your company have gone bankrupt too?"

The manager laughed. "No. We're independently funded. Wu was planning to set up a cooperative to run the fish-farm. If it had gone bust, all it would have meant is a lot of ruined people in Nanping, so we could have paid our workers less. Which would have suited me—except that I'm also a resident of this village and I know how hard people have worked to get where they are."

Wang looked carefully at the businessman. Wei seemed genuinely to mean what he was saying. "Tell me more about the contracts. Wu seems to have been undecided which one to accept."

"Ah. You *have* been doing your research! It wasn't what I expected of Wu: he was normally very decisive. But to me that showed he'd got out of his depth. In truth, there was only one serious contender."

"Who?"

"Sheng He. The other lot, Yap Seeow, are a bunch of crooks. Sheng He do a lot of business with foreigners: that means they'd charge too much, but at least the job gets done properly. Yap Seeow work for local government. Their record is appalling—except at opening 'back doors' and bribing quality-control inspectors. I wouldn't employ them to clean the toilets."

"So why the hesitation?"

"I don't know. Again, I can only guess: much against his will, Wu was having second thoughts about the whole thing. It didn't help, of course, talking the matter over with his son."

"His son?"

"Oh, yes. Wu Weidong was the only person the Secretary would discuss the matter with. Deputy Yao still wanted the work done by forced labour; I thought the whole project was crazy. What he should have done was talk with his superiors—but that was his pride again." Wei sighed. "I wrote to the Secretary several times, telling him that if he insisted on going through with this project, he had to take the Sheng He contract. He stopped replying after a while."

Wang began fiddling with a pencil from the desk in front of him.

"You've a strange expression," said Manager Wei. "What are you thinking about?"

"Do you have phone numbers for those companies?" Wang asked.

"Certainly." Wei crossed to his computer, and soon had them up on the screen. "Any other information you require, while I'm on the database?"

"The name and number of any company involved in tarmacking the road to Wentai, back in 'eighty-eight."

Manager Wei looked puzzled, but tapped his way to the information.

"What sort of company were they?" Wang asked. "Straight? Corrupt?"

"They did a fair job," Wei replied carefully.

Wang made three calls the next morning, then wrote some notes in his book, under the heading "Wu Weidong."

13

"Drink, anybody?" Wang Anming pointed to the large jug of orange juice on top of the bookshelf. "No alcohol in the house," he added. "New rule."

Old rule, actually, but new in the sense that it hadn't been in force for a while.

"That would be lovely," said Rosina. Wang nodded assent, as did the fourth dinner guest, a distant cousin called Peng.

"Good. Good." Anming poured out the drinks with a near-steady hand, then they all raised their beakers of juice in a toast. *Ganbei*!—down in one.

"So, sit down. Get comfortable."

The guests did so. Wang had to admit that his brother had done his best to make the hovel look appealing. The table was covered with a cloth; Father's old chopstick-rests had been taken out and polished; an arrangement of paper flowers stood next to the rather wobbly carousel on which food would soon be circulating. And the smells from the tiny kitchen were excellent; Anming could cook well if he put his mind to it. In Wang's eyes the scene was perfected by Rosina, in her bright-red dress, her hair bundled up at the back in the fashionable Japanese style.

"Wang Anming tells me you've been busy solving the local murder," said Cousin Peng.

"Helping the local police where possible."

"I believe they're not exactly making great strides of progress. Not enough manpower. And here's a detective from Beijing—"

"On a hard-earned holiday. Naturally, I'm doing what I can." Wang had taken an instant dislike to this individual, the rest of whose family looked down on the Wangs. They still hadn't forgiven Wang's grandmother for marrying an itinerant worker—even though the marriage had later saved them from humiliation in the new, People's China.

"You must have a theory on who's responsible, surely, Inspector?"

"The local police believe the murder to have been the work of robbers."

"And you?"

"I'm ready to assist them if they ask."

Cousin Peng frowned with disappointment. "The Secretary made enemies with this fish-farm scheme of his. I believe there was even some kind of protest group set up. I wouldn't be surprised if one of them didn't do it. There doesn't seem to be much respect for law and order nowadays." He helped himself to the last bowl of cashews, while the provider of the cashews blushed. "Mind you, the project did seem out of scale for a small village. I think Wu wanted to leave some kind of memorial to himself."

"Maybe," said Wang distantly. A thought occurred to him. "Of course, he would also have flooded a memorial." Supposing Wu had been the traitor of Snake Valley. Wouldn't that be a strong motive for him to flood the place? Had Lian Gang come to that conclusion too?

"What memorial?" said Anming.

"The one to the victims of the Snake Valley ambush."

"Oh, that thing."

"That memorial is important," Wang replied angrily. "Father said we shouldn't forget. He used to take us up there every year to pay our respects."

"We were just kids."

"Those people died for us!"

"Fifty years ago. It's history. We've got enough of that as it is." Anming turned to Rosina. "We Chinese are always looking back. Don't you think so?"

Rosina did think this, but didn't want to be disloyal to her husband. Fortunately she didn't have to say anything, as Anming didn't wait for her reply.

"That TV series, *Yellow River*, was right," he went on. "We can't become a really modern nation until we stop lugging round all those Emperors and Generals and Sages and Revolutionary Heroes and so on. It's like having a huge carrying-pole over our shoulder, weighted down at each end—"

"You can't say that!" Wang cut in furiously. "Without our history and our culture we'd be nothing better than savages."

"Are we much better, Anzhuang? Look what we did to each other in the Cultural Revolution."

"Who's *we?*" Wang snapped, then regretted the comment at once. But he was damned if he were going to lose face and retract it. "The Cultural Revolution was an attempt to abolish history and culture. It was precisely because of this that it degenerated into savagery. I'm not blaming individual Red Guards—"

"That's very good of you, tucked away in those cosy barracks—"

"If you think Army barracks are cosy—"

Rosina coughed. "Let's get the first dishes in. They smell delicious."

"Do you two always argue?" said Rosina, as they walked back through the muddy alleyways.

"Eventually," Wang replied.

"You shouldn't."

"I know. But he says such stupid things. Being provocative for no reason. He was like that at the meeting—if Baoren hadn't stepped in, he would have ended up in jail for conspiracy. Then there he was, at it again. It drives me crazy!"

"He's still your brother. He needs help, not criticism."

"He needs a kick up the arse!"

They left the old village and walked in silence across North Square. As they passed the old millstone, Wang looked at his wife, took her hand and said: "I'm sorry. Anming got the best treatment as the eldest son. That's standard practice in the countryside, so I can accept it. But I can't forgive him for wasting it all. When he says things like 'forget the past,' I just see him doing it again. Wasting. You know I get pretty angry when some of your friends criticize our country, our traditions and so on—but to hear that sort of thing from your own brother, who always got first call on reading and learning . . ."

"You were too busy hunting frogs!"

"I always wanted to learn more," Wang replied primly.

"You had fun. Anming clearly didn't, despite all those advantages." They walked a little further: the tarmac road ended, the hill began to steepen. "So who's the lucky one?"

Wang nodded.

"What Anming really needs to do is face up to his past," Rosina continued. "It's serious: if he doesn't, drink will ruin his life. You do want him to have a decent life, don't you?"

Wang thought for a moment. Did he really want that? "Yes, I do," he said finally.

Rosina kissed him. "I knew you'd say that."

"Who is it?" snapped Station Chief Huang.

"Wang Anzhuang."

"Oh. Come in. I'm afraid I'm very busy at the moment. What can I do for you?"

Wang entered. "I've come to offer my services."

"What as?"

"A simple working policeman. Nothing more."

"You want to take charge of things, do you?"

"Only if that is what the situation demands. In your judgement."

The chief grinned. "Well, I must say, we are a little short

staffed. I'm afraid Wentai has not come up with the number of officers I requested. Despite this, we are making good steady progress—but extra help would be useful. Especially on routine tasks.''

"Most policework is routine.''

"Exactly.''

"There is something I want in return.''

"Ah.'' The chief glanced round his office, his eyes ultimately falling on the duty rosters. "What?''

"I want to talk to Wu Weidong.''

"Why?''

"I need to satisfy my curiosity on certain matters.''

"Hmm.''

"It'll be just like my talk with Teacher Zhang,'' said Wang. "It won't get in the way of your investigations.'' Inside, he blanched with shame at this lie—but there was no alternative.

Huang looked at his roster again. "You're not to upset him. No accusations, no leading questions. And I take no responsibility. If he complains to me, I know nothing of this. Agreed?''

"Agreed.''

"How many hours can you spare, er, Acting Constable Wang?''

Rosina made her way carefully through the old village. This wasn't going to be easy. But nobody else could do it. Anzhuang couldn't, an outsider couldn't. Or an amateur . . . Anming had to face up to his addiction, but he also had to face up to its cause. What cause?

Rosina had some ideas, but it was up to Anming to tell her. Supposing he wouldn't? She sighed.

Left again, wasn't it? Yes. Tinker's Alley.

Anming answered the door himself. "Rosina! This is a pleasant surprise. Come in.''

They walked down the corridor, through the yard and into Anming's room. Dinner hadn't been cleared away.

"Sorry it's a bit of a mess.''

"That's OK. I'll help you sort it out.''

"No. Please sit down. Relax."

"Only if you do the same."

Anming nodded. "That was wonderful food last night," Rosina said, getting comfortable.

"I love to cook. It's just when you're on your own, you don't bother."

"You should bother."

"Why?"

"Because you have a duty to yourself."

"Do I?"

"Yes," Rosina said firmly.

"Duty's to the Party, the People, that sort of thing."

"And to yourself."

Anming paused. "Isn't that bourgeois individualism?"

"I've never understood politics. Can I have some tea?"

"Oh yes, of course." Anming scuttled off into his kitchen, from which Rosina heard the clattering of metal-ware, mutters of complaint about a tap, something falling to the floor and breaking, and finally the sound of a kettle boiling.

While Anming did battle with the tea, Rosina ran her mind over the new, western therapeutic techniques she'd studied. Forget three thousand years of *qi*, the lecturer had said; forget Maoist exhortations to right thinking. Chronically depressed people suffer from memories that need to be faced up to and re-evaluated in the company of another person. ("Just like a Struggle Meeting," an older nurse had commented drily.) Such a process wasn't easy. The unconscious mind puts up stiff resistance: patients try and change the subject, then can get abusive, even violent—

"It's nice to see you," said Anming, re-entering with two china tea mugs, one minus its lid. "I'm sorry if last night—"

"Siblings argue. Nothing wrong in that."

"No, but . . ." Anming sighed. "You're lucky to be the age you are. One, because of your looks, but also because you missed—well, all that business back in the late sixties. Anzhuang missed it too, and I don't think he really understands how lucky he was. I've no doubt that Army recruits got all the brainwashing we did—but they didn't have to go and put it into practice, in their own home villages. We did." He raised his mug to his nose, sniffed the steam and smiled. "But I shouldn't be going on about the past, should I? Not after what I said last night."

"I don't see why not. I want to get to know you better. You're my brother-in-law. And I've only got eight more days in Nanping."

"I know. I should have organized our dinner earlier—"

"Stop apologizing! It was a lovely meal. And I'm here now."

"Yes." Anming smiled. "It's nice to have someone to talk to, someone family. You know the phrase: 'Private problems must not bring public shame.' But I'm determined not to bore you!"

"It won't be boring."

"It will be. Tell me about life in Beijing."

Rosina looked at the clock on the mantelpiece. Plenty of time. So she told him about the traffic, the dust storms, the pollution, shopping on Wangfujing, the foreigners on the streets, Western-style restaurants, the company of artists and intellectuals. And about the books you could get there. And the movies by people like Chen Kaige and Zhang Yimou that won awards in the West but only urban Party members got to see in China. And about slang and fashion and silly things like the way people had started carrying replica mobile phones to impress . . .

Anming listened with the eagerness of a child, then said: "I went to Beijing once. In nineteen sixty-seven, to a Red-Guard rally in Tiananmen Square. Me and a million other sheep. Baa! Baa!"

"You should tell me about those days," said Rosina.

"Why?"

"Because you want to. I can tell."

Anming said nothing for a while. Rosina sipped her tea. Then the former Red Guard laughed nervously.

"Anzhuang is right to criticize me," he began. "I made a clear commitment to join the Red Guards, long before it became necessary for survival. I stood up for Chairman

Mao; I volunteered to go round chanting his slogans. All Imperialists are Paper Tigers! Criticize Confucius! Death to all Capitalist Roaders! And, of course, Down with the Four Olds!—the smash-up slogan, the one we used when destroying people's property or those statues on the hundred-Buddha pagoda . . . I thought Mao was going to build a new China, you see. Something better, something fairer, something stronger. Everything had to be judged by those standards: me, my friends, my family, my home, my life.''

"And love?"

Anming blushed. "Yes. Especially that. Love was for the Party, for Chairman Mao, the People and so on. Not for individuals—that was bourgeois, Western, decadent. We had to avoid what Lenin called dissoluteness; we had to keep our energies pure and strong. And we had always to remember the class struggle. Supposing a man found a woman attractive, then found out she was from one of the black classes?"

"Difficult," Rosina said slowly.

"Very difficult—for those it happened to, of course . . ." Anming fell silent again.

Rosina cursed herself for pushing too hard.

"Did my brother send you?" said Anming after a pause.

"No."

"You're sure? He's not getting at me?"

"I'm here because I want to be here. You said it: I'm family. Your family are either the people you lie to the most, or the people you trust the most. It's your choice."

Anming nodded. "Yes. I'm sorry. Where was I?"

"In love."

"Ah." The ex-fanatic's eyes roved round the room. His feet shuffled as if they wanted to bolt for the door. "Of course, I don't believe in that sort of nonsense any longer. Do you? Really?"

"Freud said that to love and to work are the two most important things we can do in our lives."

Anming looked round the room again. "I wonder which I've done worse, worked or loved."

"You shouldn't talk like that. It's defeatist."

"It's true."

"You can always change."

"Eradicate all poisonous weeds! Long live the People's Communes!"

"You can change. If you face up to the past."

Anming shook his head. "That carrying-pole. It's too heavy!"

"Put it down."

"I can't."

"You can. You have the courage. You declined the chairmanship of our group. That wasn't the act of a weak man."

"I shouldn't have got myself into that position in the first place," said Anming—but something in him had been roused. "You won't like me when I tell you this."

"I won't like you if you lie to me. Your own sister-in-law."

Anming looked at her, gave that nervous laugh again, then spoke.

"She was the daughter of the local landlord . . ."

14

Wang Anming told his story almost without pause.

"Xu Yifeng and I grew up together, but we weren't close friends as kids. Our backgrounds made that impossible— even before the Cultural Revolution there were campaigns to remind us how much class mattered: anti-rightism, Socialist education and so on. But I always liked her. She was naturally lively; I was the quiet type. Bookish, you know." He gestured round at the room, piled high with earnest, pastel-covered paperbacks from New China Publishing House.

"Of course, she'd have her down times, too. At the height of those campaigns, usually. But that was against her nature. Heaven gave her a cheerful temperament: the Son of Heaven took it away. Anyway, I liked her for those moods too. I hated girls who were pushy and jolly and sporty the whole time. Yifeng was, well, perfect." Anming blushed. "I wrote poems and sent them to her. Anonymously, of course. And I didn't even compose them, I just copied them from *A Dream of Red Mansions*. You know, that bit where they sit around in the garden writing verses for one another . . ."

Rosina tried to keep the smile off her face: the speaker's brother had done the same to her.

"I hate that book now," Anming went on. "Such sentimental drivel. Anyway, one day I summoned up the courage to speak to Yifeng. We became sort of acquaintances. Then a few weeks later we went for a walk, up the hill—there weren't any of those disgusting rich men's villas there then, just trees. She said she was afraid of me, because of politics, and I said—*aiya*, something silly like 'politics doesn't matter if you're in love.' She told me to go away and read Marx. Marx! I suppose I got angry, and we parted on bad terms." Anming shook his head. "After that, I spent hours imagining that walk over and over again, saying different things each time, producing different outcomes—all favourable, of course. Then I moved into another class and we didn't see each other. Then Father died. Then Anzhuang went away to join the Army. Then it all started: the Cultural Revolution . . ."

Anming wrung his hands. "Other generations didn't have to go through this. Father's lot could stand and fight; you younger people can have your careers and homes and things. We were used; we were lied to; we were encouraged to be vicious and destructive and hateful and mindless. Then we were chucked away because we weren't any use any longer—which we weren't, of course. No fucking use at all. No skills, no affection, no intelligence—just those bloody slogans going round and round in our heads. And a whole lot of memories of all the things we'd done. And of how much we'd enjoyed doing them . . .

"Xu Yifeng came to see me one day. Soon after it all started, soon after that TV broadcast by Lin Biao. She got down on her knees and begged me to have a word with the new Secretary, Zhang, or with Deputy Wu, or with anyone in authority. She said she'd do anything to help her family. But I'd already joined the Red Guards, so I said right away there was nothing I could do. I told her that she came from a black class, that she had to pay for the crimes of her ancestors. She began to cry. I said that if she didn't leave, I'd report her. Then she reminded me of our walk on the hillside and what I'd said about love and politics. Well, I really tore into her . . .

"She took it for a bit, then just turned round and walked out. Suddenly I wanted to run after her. But instead I looked up at the picture of Chairman Mao on the wall, and congratulated myself for my self-discipline." Wang Anming hung his head in shame. "Can you believe it? I betrayed the only woman I've ever loved, then I turned to a photograph of a mass-murderer and sought his approval. What kind of person does that make me, Rosina?"

"Millions of others made similar mistakes."

"I pity them, then. Anyway, there's more. The Xu family lived in one of those compounds out on the eastern side of the village. That's the nice side, if you hadn't guessed already. One evening there was a big march over there; we forced them to come out and be criticized. Her father, her brother, and her . . .

Then we burnt a lot of paintings and stuff. We did that to anyone who had what we called relics of the Four Olds in their homes. A few days later, we moved other people into their compound. Then we moved them out altogether, and put them in a place we called the cowshed. We made them work in the fields all day: in the evening there'd be more criticism sessions. They had to confess everything, you see. Old Xu was a real fighter; it took a lot to get anything out of him. I think that's why he was killed . . ."

Anming stared at the ground, then looked up at Rosina. "I had nothing to do with the murders, I swear. I took part in that raid on their house. We all did. And I helped march them off to the cowshed. There was a great big crowd of us. If you haven't been part of a crowd and felt its madness, you've no right to criticize—"

"I'm not criticizing."

"No . . ." Anming sighed. "The old man and the son were found beside one of the fish ponds one day, battered to death. With iron bars, apparently. I still wonder what it sounds like, an iron bar cracking someone's skull. I sometimes imagine it happening to me. Why not? If there's no justice, if a mob can do whatever they want provided they

chant the right slogans—is anyone safe? The worst thing
of all was that Xu Yifeng was arrested for the killings.
Yifeng! It was such a ludicrous charge that even Red Tiger
Zhang had to drop it. But they didn't let her out of jail;
they just invented some new offence. She was a black el-
ement, a potential saboteur, an ally of imperialism, a bourgeois revisionist—*aiya*, I could go on forever . . . She was
sent to a Reform Through Labour camp in Heilongjiang.''
He spoke the syllables of the far northern province slowly,
to emphasize their individual meanings: Black Dragon
River. ''I've got a book on that place here somewhere. In
winter it gets down to minus forty. Your skin freezes off
your face like a burn; get caught in a blizzard fifty metres
from shelter and you're dead. We Shandongers can't imagine what it's like . . . I doubt if she lasted more than a few
months.'' Anming leant forward. ''And I sent her there.''

''You can't say that.''

''Why not? I could have done something to help her.''

''You'd have brought great suffering on your family.''

''Maybe. Maybe not. Other people broke the rules and
got away with it.''

''You were a teenager. A boy.''

''I was old enough to destroy things. And people. Why
not to save people, to help people?'' Wang Anming hid his
head in his hands. ''There is justice, Rosina. Not human,
but divine. I've got what I've deserved—plus a little clemency, really. Forget loving and working, it's drinking and
surviving for me, but I'm still alive, in my home, in Shandong. I'm not a frozen carcase in a nameless prisoner's
uniform, a thousand *li* north of here. *Aiya*, no wonder the
ghosts have come back!''

''Ghosts?'' Rosina tried to keep the superiority out of
her voice. She failed.

''You don't believe in ghosts, then?''

''No. Modern science says—''

''Everyone believes in them round here.''

Rosina reminded herself that hallucinations can often affect reformed alcoholics.

Anming was on his feet. ''Thank you for listening to my

story, Rosina. I appreciate it. Very much.'' He smiled.
''Families are odd things. Every now and then they need
new blood, someone who can come in and see things in a
new light. We're very fortunate to have you.'' He paused.
''Of course, you won't tell your husband what I said, will
you?''

''You know I won't.''

''I'd rather he despised me for being weak than for being
a traitor.'' Anming grinned again, that joyless, totally Chinese grin that can cover any number of difficult emotions,
especially when they are all operating at the same time.

''I can't tell you,'' said Rosina.

''He's my brother.''

''What he said was in confidence.''

Wang scowled. But he knew she was right. ''He's ill,
you say?''

''Yes . . . Look, you must promise never to tell Anming
I told you this. On our marriage.''

''I promise.''

''He thinks he sees ghosts.''

''This is the countryside. Everyone sees ghosts. Not just
batty old men.''

''Hallucinations can be an early symptom of serious
mental collapse. Brought on by alcohol abuse. He's in trouble, Anzhuang.''

Wang sighed. ''What can we do? We can't watch over
him the whole time. Or even visit that often: Beijing's a
day's journey away.''

''Get him a course of treatment, then pay someone here
to look after him.''

''Full time?''

''No. But regularly.''

''How much would that cost?''

''Not too much. Especially by your sister's standards.''

''Ah! The female mind at work!''

''I sometimes think that's the only type of mind that does
work. She makes a fortune at that bank of hers. You must
persuade her to come up with some money.''

Wang sighed. "That won't be easy. She can be terribly mean." He took another sip of the pre-lunch cordial they had been enjoying. "Ghosts, Anming sees, does he?"

Acting Constable Wang reported for duty that afternoon.

"We've got a stake-out for you," said the chief.

Wang nodded. It was worth it.

"Meanwhile, Teacher Zhang is coming in to be interviewed. You'd better make yourself scarce."

"Yes." Wang paused. He wanted to hear this. "Do you record all interviews?" he asked.

Huang was about to say no, of course he bloody well didn't, but a voice inside warned him that the Beijing inspector might be testing him in some way. All this volunteering for service was too good to be true.

"Of course I do," he said.

A door opening. The station chief's voice. "Sit down, please. I'll try and take as little of your time as possible. As you know, we're following various leads in the matter of the untimely death of Secretary Wu . . ."

"Yes."

"We have reason to believe you were in the vicinity of the Secretary's house that evening."

"Yes."

"Why?"

"Er, I went for a walk."

"Quite a long walk, from your place of residence."

"I needed time to think about a problem. One of the children at work is—"

"Which child?"

"Er, the Fu boy. He's a bright fellow, but his parents argue a lot. He's becoming disruptive. I don't want him causing you trouble in five years" time."

A laugh. "Now, to go back to the night of the murder. What did you see while you were on the hillside?"

"Nothing."

"Nothing?"

"Well, Mr. Bo and his friend. We stopped and talked. Is that how you know I was there?"

"Never mind how we know."

"Well, it must be him, because I didn't speak to anyone else."

"Did you see anyone else?"

"No. It's quiet up there."

"And what time were you in the area?"

"From just before eight, to about quarter past nine."

"Oh. That's a long time."

"It was a beautiful evening."

"But you didn't notice anything?"

"I've said, no. I wish I had."

"Any vehicles on the road?"

A quick breath. "I don't recall."

"Think."

"Er—no."

"You're sure?"

"I said, I don't recall." Wang detected panic in Zhang's voice. Then the teacher suddenly blurted out: "What do you want me to say, Officer?"

The chief seemed as shocked as his interviewee. "Well, whatever's the truth."

A pause. "I was at the house of Zhuo Song from eight till nine."

"Visiting?"

"Giving a lesson. Mathematics. His son is a bit behind in class."

"A private lesson? For money?" said the chief, thus proving he was perfectly capable of sticking the knife in respectable people, as long as he knew they couldn't fight back.

"Yes."

Silence fell. "Thank you for your cooperation, Teacher Zhang. If you do remember any details about your journey either to or from Zhuo Song's, I'd be grateful if you'd let me know."

"I will . . ." Feet, hurrying to the door. The door closing. The station chief's voice. "Private lessons! Ha, they all join in in the end!"

15

Wang looked down at his watch. Another hour to go, and his shift would be over. It had been quite pleasant, actually—he hadn't done this sort of thing for ages. He had enjoyed watching Nanping village walk up and down Cutler's Alley; old women in black, kids playing tag, vendors, bottle collectors, a shoemaker, the coal-briquette man with his handcart and dust-blackened face. He had enjoyed watching night fall and the old, poorly lit alleyway become dark and mysterious.

The door of Courtyard Seven, however, had remained shut all the time, and there had been no sign of activity within its walls.

The Ma family, residents of the courtyard, had a long tradition of law-breaking. Most of the men had been inside—the middle boy was currently being reformed in Guangxi Province—and they were suspected of many more crimes than the local police had ever been able to prove. Needless to say, the oldest son, Ma Kai, had alibis for the evenings of all the robberies, albeit from young petty crooks. The local Neighbourhood Committee had been instructed to keep a special eye on him, and had had nothing to report.

Wang, who loathed not to use time to the full, had also been thinking about his intended confrontation with Wu Weidong. The questions, the possible answers, the counter-questions. He had them worked out now, several moves in advance, like a master of *xiangqi* chess. All he needed was to get the dead man's son alone . . .

Wang stood outside the gate of the Secretary's old villa, smoking a cigarette and fighting back his disappointment. His shift over, he'd walked up to the villa with all his moves and gambits in place; Wu Weidong was not there. The Toyota wasn't there. The place looked deserted. Had Weidong run?

Had he been tipped off? If so, by who?

"Don't invent complications," the inspector told himself. The chess master never loses sight of probability, and doesn't muddle his thoughts with outrageously unlikely outcomes—until they stop looking outrageous. "He's probably gone to Jinan to sort out his finances. And anyway, if he has run, I've got enough evidence to get Public Security there on to him. Relax . . ."

But, just like the last time he'd stood here, the inspector smoked his cigarette right down to the stub. Time. If only there were more time.

The man in the green jacket had been practising his oratory.

"Fellow fighters," he said. "Thank you for coming at such short notice. Your presence is a true sign of loyalty, of seriousness of intent."

The large crowd that had gathered in the barn gave a kind of collective purr of pleasure.

"I'm sure you know what I have to say," the orator went on. "Our protests have, so far, been ignored. Why? Because we're not forceful enough in our demands. Are we afraid? Are we just going to lie down and let our land be stolen from us?"

"No!" the audience cried.

"Yes. If we let things go on as they are. Last meeting, I suggested replacing our chairman with a new candidate.

This man, if I can call him a man, was not up to it—''

Fei Baoren, sitting with Rosina at the back, clenched her fist. ''How dare he say that!'' she muttered.

Rosina concurred. She thought of her husband saying ''Anming's always been weak'': the poor guy never got a chance.

''I'm proposing that at the next meeting, I am formally put forward as chairman,'' the orator was saying. ''I want to enlist your support, and to consult you about exactly what courses of action we should follow.''

Baoren shook her head. ''He's crazy,'' she said, a little louder than she intended.

''Ah! Did I hear some dissent at the back there?''

Silence fell.

''The lady next to the Party spy, Fei Baoren: please share your comment with the rest of us.''

Baoren froze. She filled with terror; she wanted to run or shrink or vanish into the air or . . . Then something set hard inside her. Years of persecution for her rich-peasant background. All those cross-examinations, criticisms, Struggle Meetings.

''My friend is not a Party spy,'' she said slowly, and with complete calm. ''And my comment was to her, not to you.''

The man was clearly infuriated by his failure to humiliate her. An opponent and a mere woman. ''If you haven't got the guts to speak up . . .'' he snarled.

''I'll say what I want, to whom I want, when I want.''

''Huh!'' For a moment, he was beaten. But he couldn't be beaten, he had to fight back. ''Where's your father this evening, Fei Baoren?''

''Not well.''

''He looked all right the other day when I saw him at work. I wonder if he isn't losing some of his enthusiasm for our cause. He used to be such a keen supporter. Perhaps you're not the only member of your family to be spending more time in the company of Party members—''

''How dare you?'' Baoren snapped, her calm gone at once. 'My father has done more for this group than a jumped-up little nobody like you. The effort has worn him out, and he now needs a rest.''

"A rest subsidized by the Party? I happen to know that someone in our group has been making overtures to our masters. Treachery is in the air!''

Baoren looked distraught. Her father would never betray the group. But she knew that once people believed something . . . She began to stammer a defence.

"Not so confident now, eh?'' the orator began, but before he could continue, a new voice had joined the debate. Male, shaky but driven by anger. It belonged to Wang Anming. 'Fei Zhaoling has been a loyal supporter of our cause since the beginning,'' he said, dragging himself to his feet. "What right have you got to insult him like this? Behind his back, without the tiniest piece of evidence?'' He turned to the people. "Is this the kind of leader you want?''

"Yes!'' cried someone.

"At least he'll stand and fight,'' said someone else.

Anming nearly slumped into his seat—but other voices began to take his side. It soon became clear that opinion in the old barn was divided.

"You should apologize,'' said Anming, once the tumult had died down. The orator, reckoning that at least half the audience would condemn him if he didn't and that the other half were his natural supporters anyway, turned to Baoren and said: "I apologize.''

"You take those comments back? Every word?''

"Yes,'' the orator said grudgingly. "Till I get more evidence,'' he added under his breath.

The meeting continued.

When it was over, Baoren went to thank Anming.

"It was only right after what you did for me last time,'' said the old Party Secretary's son. "And anyhow, I can't stand injustice.''

"No . . .'' said Baoren.

Rosina thought that maybe the two brothers weren't so dissimilar after all. But try telling her husband that.

• • •

It was the only bright idea Wang had had all day. The station chief had told him the address where Teacher Zhang had gone to give his private lesson; five minutes talk with the pupil's father would corroborate the teacher's story (or cast huge suspicion on him). He'd still be home before Rosina came back from her meeting.

Even by night the villa was easy to find. Wang opened the gate, marched up the path and pressed a buzzer.

"Who is it?" said a mechanical voice.

"Police."

"Can you come back tomorrow?"

"No."

Pause.

"Very well."

Zhuo Song's hallway had bright-pink linoleum. On one wall was a huge bas-relief of Hangzhou's West Lake in what looked like bone and mother-of-pearl but was probably plastic. A boy peered round a corner at the new arrival.

"It's the cops!" he said, then pointed a toy pistol at Wang. "Bam! Bam!"

"Stop that, Hu," said a voice. "Go and finish your homework. Sorry, Officer. Come into the main room . . ."

"I'll be brief," said Wang. "As you know, we're looking into the murder of Secretary Wu. I'm currently checking the stories of all people who were in the area the night of the murder, Wednesday the twenty-fourth."

Zhuo Song thought for a moment. "I was at home all evening. With my family."

"I believe that you employed the local schoolmaster, Zhang Hong, to give your child an extra math lesson."

"Yes, of course. It was his evening. He can vouch for me."

"What time was he here?"

"From eight till nine. I know that's late for the boy, but Teacher Zhang is a busy man." Zhuo smiled. "He's very good, you know. Hu was way down in the class, and now he comes top almost every time. I've recommended Zhang to several friends in Nanping. And Weipowan, too. He's getting quite a reputation in the area. I know about his family and his past. But we all think he's put that behind him. And kids have to get ahead nowadays . . .''

Constable Kong was on the late watch. He got no pleasure at all from watching the same bloody people going up and down Cutler's Alley. Most of the folk out late were up to no good, even the old codgers. And as for the kids . . . The old village by night was sinister and threatening, a place where innocent people got hurt or robbed. And the Ma family appeared to be in a state of siege.

At that moment, the door of No. 7, the house under surveillance, opened, just wide enough to let a thin figure emerge. Male? Female? Kong couldn't tell. The constable picked up the shortwave radio he'd been given, fiddled with it, got a hissing noise and chucked it into a corner. Follow in person, the only way.

The figure was heading for the main street—it was carrying something—then it turned right, out towards the fields. The constable felt his pulse race, but cursed at the same time. The fields were crisscrossed with raised pathways, bumpy raised pathways that people never used at night without illumination. But he had to follow.

They were out of the village, now. And there was so little light. The weather had turned cloudy, there were no stars and only the ghost of a moon.

Don't lose them.

Don't get too close, and give yourself away.

Aiya! Constable Kong tripped on a jutting stone and tumbled down a bank into a bed of wheat-stubble. He kept his mouth shut, just: some pride at least was saved.

"So this is where Kong lost him?" said Wang, as he and the station chief walked out across the fields next morning.

"Yes."

The inspector was genuinely glad he hadn't had to follow anyone across this chequerboard, and tried to look sympathetic. "Not an easy job," he added, looking ahead.

The fields continued level for a few hundred yards, then

the sides of the valley began to rise, at first through those man-made contours that seem to be engraved on to every hill in peasant China, then into rock-faces. The only obvious place the fugitive could have been headed for was a tumble-down barn at the foot of the slope.

"That's the old Li-clan temple, isn't it?" said Wang.

"Yes."

"What's it used for now?" Before 1949, any clan of any size would have a temple to its ancestors. After the Revolution, Mao had ordered these to be gutted and put to more practical, public use.

"A maize store," the chief replied. "We've already checked it; he's not hiding there."

"He wasn't when you last looked. I think you should do so again."

The chief grunted. Wang wasn't sure if this meant yes or no, but marched off towards the building anyway.

The old temple retained few traces of its former splendour. The carved, multilayered eaves had lost all their paint and were rotting. The tiles—which would have been expensive ceramics in blue or orange—had been taken away and replaced with plastic sacking. Only one horned monster remained from the troop that once guarded the roof-ridge, a solitary sentinel abandoned by a retreating army. The door, once fine latticework, was now a rectangle of cheap timber. It was padlocked.

"We haven't got a key," said the chief, with a trace of pleasure in his voice.

"Who has?"

"Cui Shaobing."

"Your Head of Agriculture," Wang replied at once. "Anyone else?"

"A couple of local farmers—I'm not sure which ones, though."

Wang felt for the key-picks in his pocket, then said: "You put the pressure on, I'll kick."

"That's vandalism!"

"This is a murder investigation."

Station Chief Huang put all his weight on the door; his

urban colleague aimed a hard *wushu* kick at the wood just by the padlock's plate; the combination of the two kinds of pressure pulled the screws from the wood, leaving the lock hanging unconquered but useless. The door slewed open.

There was silence. The chief looked through the crack by the hinges, to check that Ma Kai wasn't lurking behind it.

"He's not here," said Huang.

"Let's look anyway," came the irritatingly undaunted reply.

The store had the sharp dry smell of dust. Maize-cobs hung from the rafters like bats or lay piled up on lattice shelves like ammunition. Nothing seemed to have been disturbed for months.

"What are those for?" Wang asked, pointing at some iron rings set in the walls.

"Oh, they're from the Cultural Revolution. This was the cowshed."

Wang grimaced. "Did they attach people to them, or cows?"

"Both. But not at the same time."

Wang began pulling at any uneven flagstones. None gave. He shone a torch round at the once-bright rafters, now grey with spiders" webs. He crawled under the lowest maize-shelf. He bashed at the wall-timbers: one came away.

"Anything there?"

"Yes. Come and look at this."

The chief got down on his stomach, and began to crawl. "Oof! I'm stuck . . . No, I'm not . . . Hang on . . . Right, what is it?"

"There's a cavity behind this timber. Look."

"So? It's empty."

"Someone thin could get in easily. It seems to run down the whole length of the wall. It might go further . . ."

"It might do. Then again, it might not. You don't seriously think Ma Kai has been hiding in there?"

"I don't know," Wang replied. He did know that, as a prime suspect of the local police, Ma Kai must be a very frightened young man. He knew that if he, Wang, were in charge of the investigation, he'd have a dog into the hiding place as soon as possible (and a watch kept on it every minute till the dog arrived). But he wasn't in charge, and he didn't believe in Ma Kai's guilt, and he had an interest in seeing the young man stay free for as long as it took him to corner Wu Weidong, for the mysterious Mr. Lian to return and for any other line of suspicion to exhaust itself.

"Can't see it myself," said the chief. "We've doubled the watch on that courtyard: next time we'll get the little bastard." The local man began turning himself round, nearly booting his colleague in the face as he did so. "I can't waste any more time here. You may get decent manpower allocations in Beijing; out here we're starved. Deliberately, in my view. None of the big-city cops want to live in the country. It's a scandal. Oof! *Aiya*! Can you push a bit? I'm stuck again. Just temporarily, of course . . ."

16

Ma Kai stared out of the bus window as it pulled in to a halt. The usual crowd of vendors surrounded it—teasing one of their number, on whom a big-nose had thrown up a few days ago.

That'll be me probably, he told himself. Scraping a living, selling crappy food or shit souvenirs; imploring people to buy them, like a dog.

He shook his head. If he could get the bastard who'd set him up . . .

But he couldn't. So he'd got a mate to take him on his bike into Wentai, and now he was on this bus, bound for Jinan.

A vendor shouted in his ear. Ma Kai told him to fuck off. The guy didn't even answer back. No, the young man said to himself, I won't be like that. I'll be tough. I'll join a Triad—they're real men. For a moment, a smile crossed his face: he'd have proper brothers, not like the crowd back in Nanping, none of whom had had the guts to join in his robberies. He'd get rich. And he'd find a decent woman again, someone with brains as well as a good body. Ma Kai hated the stupid conversation of the slags who hung round the Nanping snooker hall. One day, maybe, he'd come back to Nanping, and buy one of those villas . . .

The thought of villas led him back to the murder he was supposed to have committed, and the thought of Nanping to the family he had left behind. He'd miss them. Little brother, Mum and Dad—

"No," he muttered to himself. He'd never see them again, because the "dogs"—the cops—would kill him if he went back. So he should start getting used to the fact. Now. Ahead, in the state capital, a new family would be waiting. One he could choose for himself. He'd find out who the hardest guys were and join them. There would be tests, of course, but he'd pass them. *Mei wenti*, no problem—

A sudden hushing of the conversation on the bus broke into Kai's thoughts and made him look up. A policeman was getting on the bus. A fucking dog . . .

Ma Kai's stomach seemed to melt with terror.

Be calm, he told himself. This was the first test.

The bastard was walking down the aisle, looking each passenger in the face. Looking for . . . Well, it was obvious, wasn't it?

The terror seemed to spread to his whole body. It transfixed him, stranger and more powerful than any of those drugs he'd tried. The dog was approaching, row by row, innocent aggrieved face by innocent aggrieved face.

Keep calm.

No. If I stay, I'm dead.

Suddenly Ma Kai was on the window ledge, then rolling in the dust beside the bus. People had begun to shout; he was on his feet and running. Someone tried to stop him; he thumped the fucker in the ribs. The rest kept out of his way. If he could just make the wall ahead of him . . .

A shot rang out. Ma Kai felt a stab of pain in his leg, and his balance deserted him. He fell, then someone was upon him, then several people.

"Bastards!" he screamed, then his head was forced into the dirt.

• • •

Wang was getting used to the walk across to the villa where Secretary Wu had lived: as used as he was getting to finding nobody in.

He swore, and stood fretting outside the gate—now that Ma Kai was under arrest, time was even tighter. He reached into his pocket for his cigarettes, but the packet was empty; he walked up the dirt-track to its end, then back again, hands in pockets, mind deep in thought. And when he reached the gate again, he opened it and walked up the path.

The lock, he recalled, was easy to pick. He was in the house in an instant.

It all seemed oddly familiar. Neither Wu Weidong nor his partner had done anything to change it, apart from removing the rug on which the Secretary had died. He went upstairs, and opened the desk again. Someone had removed the papers—no doubt the chief, who would have handed the official ones on to Old Yao. Nothing new had replaced them. The bedroom was blandly empty. Wang found some clothes inside the cupboard, including those that Wu Weidong and Francine had worn at the Memorial Meeting: he breathed a sigh of relief at this discovery; they hadn't fled for good, surely.

Secretary Wu had had a telephone in his front room. Wang went down there and dialled Beijing.

Wheels Chai was at his desk.

"Hello, Anzhuang," he said. There was no enthusiasm in his voice.

"No news, I take it?"

"Yes. We've now got five hundred and eighty-four Lian Gangs. None fought in Shandong. And Sergeant Han Haotong might as well not exist."

"No . . ." said Wang.

"You don't sound surprised."

"I know you've tried your best. Can you get a couple of phone numbers for me? Wu Weidong's in Jinan. You said he'd moved into a smart new apartment. It should have a phone. And the number of his employer."

"Phone numbers? All you want is phone numbers? It *is* my lucky day." Wang heard the clicking of keys in the background. "By the way," Wheels went on, his voice much lighter now, "your assistant nearly crashed the entire system on Friday."

"Constable Lu?"

"That's the guy. He can't explain now. He says he was doing a routine enquiry and 'pressed the wrong button.' "

"That sounds like Lu. He's a very useful fellow in a fight."

"Providing you remind him who to hit. Here we are. Phone numbers are easy . . ."

Wang rang the Jinan state government maintenance department first. No, Wu Weidong wasn't there. He had asked for compassionate leave. Terrible business; his father was murdered, you know. By a thief, apparently. What the hell are the police doing nowadays? At least in Chairman Mao's time law-abiding people could sleep in their beds at night . . .

From the apartment there was no answer.

Wang went up to the office again, and searched for any hints. Nothing. He went through the drawers downstairs. Nothing. He tried the bedroom, the pockets of the clothes, the—

There was the sound of a car engine on the road outside. And of tyres, scrunching to a halt. Wang crossed to the office window, and peeped out. The blue Toyota.

Wang could have wished the interview were under slightly different circumstances, but his pleasure at Wu Weidong's return outweighed any such feelings. This pleasure increased when he saw that the young man was alone. He left the office and crossed to the bedroom, which had a large casement window that gave out on to a lawn. A drop of about twelve feet, no problem for a man like Wang. As he unfastened the latch, he heard a key scratch in the door; as his window creaked open, the front door opened too; as he climbed on to the sill—

Wang heard a great cry of anguish.

For a moment, he thought of abandoning his plan and rushing straight down to see what the problem was, but he thought better of it, scrambled out on to the ledge and jumped.

Five minutes later, Wu Weidong heard a knock at his door.

"Wang Anzhuang, isn't it?" said the young man on answering, brushing his eyes with a handkerchief. "Old Uncle Wang's son? Yes, come in. I'm sorry, I've only just got in. Come through here. Have a seat."

Wang did as he was asked. His host sat down too. "It's a terrible loss," Wang began. Not one of his planned opening gambits—but the real chess master is the one who throws all the plans away after the first move. And still wins.

"Yes," said Wu Weidong. There was almost infinite sadness in his voice. If Wang hadn't known what he did know . . .

"It takes time to get over that kind of loss," Wang said. 'My father died thirty years ago, and I still think of him. Especially coming back here, of course."

"Yes . . ." Wu Weidong replied slowly, staring vacantly ahead of him as he did so. Wang looked round at where the eight paintings had been. If this man was guilty, where were they now? He'd soon find out . . .

"Our parents did a lot for the village," Wu Weidong went on. "And you've gone off to Beijing and made a success of your time in the police. I'm afraid I've done nothing with my life."

"You've achieved something," Wang replied. "You have a nice motor car! My wife has started nagging me about getting one."

Wu Weidong grinned with embarrassment.

"I know how you got it," Wang went on.

Wu Weidong looked surprised, but only for a moment. Then his face fell—and then began to fill with relief, a passive, accepting kind of relief, that Wang had often seen in wrongdoers about to be confronted with the truth.

"Your father gave it to you, didn't he, Weidong? And he got it as a kickback from the company that tarmacked the Wentai road, back in 'eighty-eight."

"Yes . . ."

"You asked him to do that, didn't you? Played the dutiful son, in need of a reward. Even though you knew it was against his principles."

Wu Weidong nodded. Wang fell silent, sensing that the Secretary's son was struggling with things he wanted to say. He was right.

"My father wasn't an easy man. He had a short temper, and once he'd set his mind on something, that was it . . . He drove my mother and sister into a kind of exile. I deserved something for sticking with him. And I needed it. That bloody job he got me, in Jinan. It got me nowhere."

"You managed to impress Francine—"

"*Aiya!* Don't mention her. Father was right. She just wanted my connections and my money."

"I've never thought whores any less honourable than the people who patronize them."

Wu Weidong just shook his head.

"You took out a big loan not long ago, didn't you?" Wang went on.

"Yes."

"In anticipation of another big pay-off to your father, which he would then pass on to his greedy, demanding but one-and-only son?"

"Yes."

"A pay-off from the Yap Seeow Construction Company, Shanghai. I had a word with the boss, Mr. Yip."

Wu Weidong hung his head, then looked up at Wang with real fear in his eyes.

"Don't worry," the inspector went on, "I didn't threaten him. He's a practical man, not a gangster." Wang couldn't suppress a laugh. "So practical, that he offered me a retainer when I get back to Beijing. I was tempted, too. I know what it's like to want to spend cash on a woman. But I'm afraid Rosina and I will still be going to the Great Wall by coach for the foreseeable future."

"And I'll be going to jail, I suppose."

"That depends. We haven't finished the story. Mr. Yip didn't know about your father's death; he was getting worried about the contract. He hadn't heard from your father for a while. His rival, Mr. Li at Sheng He, didn't know about the death either, but was in a much better mood. Your father had had extensive discussions with him recently; as far as he was concerned the contract was as good as signed. But of course he didn't offer me a bribe. Any more than he offered your father one. So things weren't looking good for your kickback."

Wu Weidong had a new expression on his face. Horror. Wang fell silent, and watched this expression grow in intensity.

"You can't think . . ." Wu Weidong croaked at length. "You don't . . . You do. You bastard!" And he launched himself at the inspector in a torrent of oaths and fists.

Fights between Army veterans who practise several forms of martial art and unfit office workers tend to be brief, and this one was no exception. Wu Weidong was soon back in his chair, weeping like a baby—with fear and humiliation, not physical pain, which had not been necessary.

"A young man is at this moment being interrogated for the murder," said Wang, once Wu Weidong had recovered sufficiently to pay attention. "Station Chief Huang will use rather more obvious methods than me. An innocent man will then be shot. I want the truth."

"I didn't kill my father," said Wu Weidong.

"Prove it."

"I was at home with Francine that evening."

"Just the two of you?"

"Yes."

"Your accomplice? That's not a very good alibi."

Wu Weidong pondered. "If I swear on my honour . . ."

"Not worth much, after one successful and one attempted scam."

"No." Wu Weidong sighed. "Well, you might as well arrest me. I'm innocent, but I've nothing much to live for now. I'd have to sell the car to pay off the debt on the flat. I'd lose my job. And despite what you said about Francine,

I did love her . . .'' He held out his hands, as if to have cuffs put on them.

Wang studied his checkmated opponent very carefully before he spoke. "I haven't the power to arrest you," he said finally. "I'm merely an interfering holidaymaker. And you won't lose your job if you just turn up at the office next Monday. And I think you'll get over Francine: you weren't exactly quick to leap to her defence when I questioned her honour. You might even find a better wife if you try earning an honest living."

A little voice in the inspector muttered "some hope!," of Wu Weidong going straight or of that paying matrimonially. But he silenced it.

17

Wang sat on the verandah again, watching the sun go down and filling in his book.

"So it's not Wu Weidong," said Rosina, looking over her shoulder.

"Not if I'm any judge of character."

"Or Francine," she added, with disappointment.

"Unlikely. Not now she has an alibi."

"So it's our Mr. Lian."

"Who is one of five hundred and eighty-four. And counting."

"Who else is in your book?"

"Next page? Teacher Zhang. There was something odd about him when I went to see him. But I don't think it was him." Wang told his wife about his suspicions, then the interview with Station Chief Huang.

She listened. "He didn't like Secretary Wu, though, did he?"

"No. But I don't see . . ." Then Wang fell silent.

"You must confess!" said Station Chief Huang.

"I can't," Ma Kai replied.

"You can. And will."

The boy stayed silent. He'd lasted a day and a night now. How much longer could he hold out?

"I don't think you understand the severity of the charges, Ma Kai. The robberies are serious enough in themselves, but murder . . . Your only chance of avoiding a bullet in the head is to make a full, frank confession. Soon."

"I didn't kill anyone."

"You did the robberies, right?"

"No."

"You're lying."

"I said no." But even Ma Kai could feel the desperation in his voice. Perhaps he should confess to the robberies. At his age he'd probably only get a few years Reform Through Labour, especially if he came clean straight away. But this other charge . . .

"Don't lie to me," said Huang. "It doesn't pay. You're gambling with your life here."

"I'm innocent," said Ma Kai weakly. More weakly than the other times.

The police chief sat back in his seat. He'd reel this lad in like a fish, crime by crime.

The official from the Pest Control Department walked across the fields to the Zhang compound and stood outside the door ringing the bell.

"There's no one in," said a passing neighbour.

I know, Wang thought. "Oh," he said, "that's a shame. We've had a complaint about rodent infestation, and we're checking some of the houses here."

"Teacher Zhang is at the school all day, and his wife won't be back till midday."

Wang feigned annoyance. The neighbour walked on.

When there was nobody around, Wang took out his key-picks, selected the most appropriate one and pushed it into the lock. The tumbrils clicked open, then it was just a matter of turning the handle.

The pile of comics was still up on the shelf of the main room. Wang took them down. There was no dust on the top, but this didn't mean much, as the room was spotlessly clean. He began to read.

Assuming Charge was about Vietnam, the war that Wang had fought in. Not America's Vietnam war, but China's, the one fought in 1979 over border country in the Guangxi and Yunnan provinces. Wang still didn't trust the Viets: they had their eyes on the Spratly Islands, which, of course, belonged to China.

"The men lined up for the attack, patriotic zeal and love of the Party filling their hearts . . ."

Wang had read these things as a boy, and they'd filled him with martial dreams. The reality of war, he'd learnt, was very different. Yet he still couldn't read the comic without a tug of emotion. Anger, at their dishonesty, or a secret longing for the world they portrayed? Anyway, no characters had been cut out of the text.

Wang began *Death or Glory*. Who in the Zhang family read such stuff? Nobody, surely. So they'd been confiscated from peasant boys who found them more fun than lessons. But why bring them back here?

He checked through them all. Not a character missing. Wang unlocked the teacher's desk.

"Aha! Scissors and paste." He riffled through some papers. "A writing pad." He took some of the paste, and smeared it on a sheet of writing paper. He also examined the blade of the scissors and made a cut in the paper, which he then folded up and put in his pocket. "I'll get one of those hate-letters off Huang, and send them up to Beijing for analysis. Shouldn't take more than a couple of days to get a result, if I pull enough strings . . ."

Wang glanced at his watch. A quarter to twelve. Time to go.

Rosina was getting to know the backstreets of the old village pretty well. She found Tinker's Alley with no problem, and knocked confidently on the door of Courtyard Four. Anming answered in person, smiling.

"Come in," he said, shepherding her into the courtyard.

"I've made some food for you. Just *jiaozi*, but with lots of different fillings."

He showed her into his bedsit. "I'll get some tea, as well."

Rosina looked round at the room. It was genuinely tidy—for her, or because Anming had gained some self-respect?

"I thought what you did at the meeting was very honourable," said Rosina.

"It was the least I could have done," Anming replied from the kitchen: his home was so small that you didn't need to raise your voice to talk from any part of it to any other. "And, as I said, I hate injustice. I don't like Fei Zhaoling, and he doesn't like me—but he's no traitor to our cause."

"You don't like him?" said Rosina with a trace of disappointment in her voice.

"No. He's so bitter about the past. That's typical of what I was talking about the other day." Anming returned with a plate of half-moon dumplings, some vinegar dip and two mugs on a tray (one of which now had a tin lid). "All these things that happened a generation ago. People don't forget . . ." He put the tray down. "*Aiya*, I don't blame them. We are the ones who should be setting an example, the ones who did the damage. Not patching up memorials. Why should Fei Zhaoling forget what happened to him and his family? I think they ought to knock that obelisk down and put up a new one, to all the people killed in the Cultural Revolution and the Great Leap Forward and all the other bloody silly political campaigns ordinary people have had to suffer over the years."

Anming stopped, suddenly embarrassed.

"Don't tell Anzhuang, but I rather agree," said Rosina.

Anming grinned. "Have a dumpling." He watched her eat. "I made them all myself. D'you like it?"

"Yes."

"Good." Anming frowned. "Now, I suppose you want to go on digging into my past. Where were we?"

"Talking about a ghost."

"Ah. Yes. You must think I'm a real hick."

"No."

"Shit-shovellers, they call us in the cities, don't they?"

"I don't." Rosina helped herself to another dumpling.

"It was only a kind of ghost."

"What kind?"

"A living one. A person. But something sent her, it had to. Something malevolent, vindictive, powerful and all-seeing. That's either the Communist Party or Yama, King of Hell!" Anming laughed at his joke; Rosina nodded.

"So our ghost is female," she said.

"Yes. And looks exactly like Xu Yifeng."

"Ah. And what did she do to you?"

"Asked questions. About the Cultural Revolution. Over and over again. What did I remember? What did I do? Who with, and to whom?" He gave a gesture of helplessness. "Can you imagine what it felt like? Remembering these things, in her presence. It was a judgement, it had to be. A hellish judgement."

Rosina shuddered. The old Buddhist hell was a place where vicious torture was an art, and it still lurked in the Chinese imagination—even for the most urban and sophisticated individual. "Why did you let her?" she said.

"Don't know. It was a chance to see Yifeng again. To feel—well—desire. And I felt I deserved the pain it caused. And she was doing important work, of course."

"What work?"

"Academic research. Into economics. At Fudan University. I checked her out with the police after her first visit, and she was quite genuine. Her name was Ping Li, and she was doing a doctoral thesis comparing economic development in two Shandong villages."

"Why did she choose to talk to you?"

"I was chosen at random off a computer printout. She wanted a cross section of Nanping society, and I was one of the people it chose from what she called Group Four. Group One is rich, Group Five destitute."

Rosina winced. "And she was nothing to do with the Xu family?"

"I asked her about her home, and she said she lived in

Shanghai. Well, you could tell from the accent, all soft and snake-like. I even checked up on her mother's maiden name. It was Cong. Not Xu. But to look at her . . ."

"It's a strange coincidence," said Rosina.

Anming shook his head. "No coincidence. Judgement. Justice. A warning." He looked at his sophisticated, capital-city visitor and said without a trace of irony: "Yama, King of Hell, sent her to tell me I'm on his list unless I lead a better life."

Wang and Rosina were on the verandah again, enjoying the view.

"What d'you know about identification?" she asked suddenly.

"A lot," Wang replied.

"Good. You can tell me how accurate it is."

"By trained or untrained witnesses?"

"Untrained."

"Appalling. By and large people see what they expect to see, or what they want to see."

"Which?"

"It depends. In the classic witness situation, where people are simple observers of some incident, expectation is the key factor. If they're personally involved, emotions tend to take over. Of course, one can't make a watertight distinction. Prejudice, for example, is a mixture of expectation and emotion. The number of crimes reported as being done by tall Manchurians that end up having been committed by ordinary-size Beijingers . . ."

"What about identification of particular individuals?"

"Same story. As long as the perpetrator has one or two traits in common with the individual we expect or want it to be, we'll make up the rest. Especially over time, as memory recycles the incident . . . Why are you asking?"

"Nothing."

"That means 'something.' Is it Anming's ghost?"

"No!"

"It's Anming's ghost. Who looked like . . ." Then Wang's voice died.

Rosina said nothing, and the conversation appeared to stop. Wang went back to *The Water Margin*, Rosina to her pirated copy of *Half of Man Is Woman*. Then Wang said: 'The ghost was young and female, wasn't it?''

"*Aiya*! My mother was right about marrying a police-man."

"You must tell me the truth. I know there's an issue of confidentiality, but he is my brother. We're both committed to helping him. And there could be other ramifications, too."

"Other?"

Wang took out his little black book. "Red Tiger Zhang is dead, so Secretary Wu was the most senior official from the days of the Cultural Revolution still alive. When I think of what Xu Yifeng's family went through in those days, it makes my blood boil. What would it do to a relative? You must tell me as much as you can."

Rosina did so. When she had finished, Wang scribbled in his book. Rosina looked out over the roofs of Nanping and hated this place, with its violence and petty-mindedness.

18

Station Chief Huang beamed with pleasure. "We're making good progress. Ma Kai has admitted to the four robberies prior to the murder."

Wang tried to hide his reaction.

"We are meeting some resistance on the latter confession, but nothing to be worried about. Once people begin to admit their crimes . . ."

They often end up confessing to things they haven't done, Wang thought. "He'll be shot, won't he?" he said.

The chief looked taken aback. "Of course! We're civilized out here: we don't torture people to death. Even people who kill Party officials. A quick bullet in the neck, and that's done. Society freed from yet another dangerous individual."

"And if he were just guilty of robbery?"

"He isn't. But if he was, then I guess he'd be in line for reforming."

Wang nodded. "I've a couple of favours to ask you."

"Ask away," said the happy, successful station chief.

The first, an example of the hate-mail that Secretary Wu had received, was easy. As was the second.

"Ping Li, postgraduate student, Fudan University,

Shanghai," said the chief, reading off a record card in one
of his filing cabinets. "Age, twenty-five. Status, single."
He chuckled. "Probably looked like a horse: these intellectuals do. She came here in May, stayed for four weeks."

"So there's no picture of her?"

"No."

"Where did she stay?"

"At Yang's, like everyone else does. Apart from VIPs,
of course."

Yang's Boarding House was for Chinese citizens only—
Nanping's rare overseas visitors had to head on up the hill
to Mrs. Ming and pay in US dollars. Luxurious it was not,
but the Yangs kept it clean, which was an improvement on
most rural travellers' accommodation. Wang found Mr.
Yang sitting at Reception, filling in a ledger and cleaning
his teeth with a piece of wood.

"Miss Ping? Nice girl. Quiet. Paid her bills with no fuss.
She was on some kind of college grant. Can't see why
anyone would want to research Nanping, but she said we'd
been in the papers."

"Did she remind you of anyone?" Wang asked.

"Not really."

"Nobody local?"

"No."

Wang cursed under his breath. "How well do you remember the Xus?" he asked finally: the worst type of questioning, the kind that lawyers were now beginning to tear
to pieces whenever they had the chance. But he didn't have
an alternative.

"Who?"

"The landlords, back in the old days."

"Don't remember them."

"Miss Ping didn't remind you of anyone from the old
days, then?"

"No," Yang replied. "Mind you, I don't have much
memory for faces. Names, of course, I can remember. We
had a chap called Zhuang Zhuangzhuang stay here
once . . ."

"Fudan University registry. Can I help you?"

"I want information on one of your students, please."

"Our records are confidential."

Wang paused. He didn't want Ping Li to know the police were after her. "My name is Guo Lingyang. I'm a professor at Chengdu University. Criminology department. I only have a brief request. She's a postgraduate student, female, name of Ping Li. I need a home and a current address for her."

"We can't give that sort of information out on the phone. What course is she studying?"

"Economics."

"You can always try contacting her at the appropriate department."

"Do you have the name of her tutor?"

Computer keys tapped. "Professor Xiao."

"That's very useful . . . That is Miss Ping Li from Heilongjiang province, isn't it?"

"That's not what it says here. But I can't give you an address. Sorry."

"Department of economics."

"Professor Xiao, please."

"He's in a seminar at the moment."

"When will he be finished?"

"Twelve." Pages rustled. "Then he has a lecture."

"Can I catch him at lunch?"

"He has tutorial groups twelve till two, then a delegation from Inner Mongolia are coming . . . He doesn't seem to be a very easy man to get hold of, I'm afraid."

"No. Do you know a Ping Li? Postgraduate student, female."

"No. She's one of his students, is she? I don't really know them. I've not been in the job long."

"Ah. Can I speak to someone she does classes with?"

"I don't know who she does classes with. She may not even do classes. A lot of the postgraduates don't."

"Haven't you got lists?"

"I haven't. Have you tried registry?"

"Yes," Wang said halfheartedly.

There was only one way to do this properly, anyway.

It took the best part of a day to get to Shanghai. Jeep to Wentai, bus to Jinan, train down the main line—the last hundred miles through a kind of perpetual building site. If Nanping thought it was booming . . . Now, after a night at a flea-ridden hotel that made him dream of staying at Yang's, Wang was sitting on an articulated bus with about a hundred and fifty students. Some were holding hands, all were talking—not, as Wang expected, about love and the meaning of life, but about timetable clashes and a new coffee bar. Perhaps Shanghai's premier university wouldn't be so intimidating after all.

He still wasn't looking forward to telling anyone he was a policeman, but there was no other way of opening the right doors. We make all this possible, the inspector reminded himself, glancing out at a young man with rebel-length hair swinging a bag of books. A society that had no law or order wouldn't bother with education. Look at the Cultural Revolution, when all colleges and universities closed down.

These thoughts made Wang's first sight of the university compound all the more surprising: in the middle was a huge concrete statue of Chairman Mao. Such idols had once filled China but were now extremely rare. Why had this particular one been allowed to stand? Mao had hated intellectuals: was this a kind of warning to the inmates, to remember their place? Or was the thing just so solid that the college couldn't afford to take it down? One thing was certain: the lad playing catch by bouncing a tennis ball off the Chairman's bottom would have been taken out and shot twenty years ago. Wang found himself smiling at the youngster's casual iconoclasm.

"Professor Xiao is busy," snapped the receptionist.

"I only want a few minutes of his time," Wang replied gently.

"So do about a dozen other people."

Wang gave a sigh of regret and produced his police ID.

"I'll just go and get him, Inspector."

"Ping Li. One of our best students. She's not in any kind of trouble, is she?"

"No, but we do need to interview her urgently. She might have been a witness to a serious crime." People still fell for that old one. Even, it seemed, economics professors.

"She's in Shandong province at the moment. Wushui village."

Wang had never heard of it, and asked the professor to locate it for him on a map. It was deeper in the uplands than Nanping, but not so far that a motorbike or moped couldn't make the journey. And the approach to Nanping was from the north, across the pass, not along the road. So nobody in the village would see her on her way to the Secretary's villa.

Wang told himself not to jump to conclusions, and asked for more details about Ping's research topic.

"The effect of the Cultural Revolution on economic growth," the professor answered. "Li reckons that the more fanatical the Red-Guard activity in an area, the better the subsequent growth."

"Oh," said Wang.

"It's an ingenious theory—albeit rather tactless to us oldies. She reckons Mao cleared out a lot of dead wood, enabling young, dynamic entrepreneurs to flourish in the subsequent decade. It's a bit like the Second World War—compare the economic performances of Germany, Japan and Britain."

"I see."

"Can't see the evidence for it myself . . ." And the professor who couldn't spare anyone a second of his time went off into a long description of various studies undertaken over recent years, their methodologies, problems with sampling errors, reliability of information and something called stochastic variation which seemed to cause no end of trouble.

"Have you got her address?" Wang asked at the end of it.

"Oh, yes." The professor tapped into a computer on his desk. "Main Street, Wushui. Only street, Wushui, I think."

"And her home address?"

More taps. "Flat Forty-nine, Building Twelve, Hong Kou Park. Nice part of town."

"Do they have a telephone?"

"Home and work numbers for both parents," said the professor, and read them out. "If you want to contact Wushui, you have to call Party HQ. It's the only telephone in the village."

A machine in the corner began humming. "Ah, that's the fax I've been expecting from London. You must excuse me, Inspector."

Wang got to Hong Kou Park early—he'd called and made an appointment to meet Ping Li's mother—and killed the time contemplating the memorial to the writer Lu Xun that stands there: a bust of the author and an inscription on the plinth in Chairman Mao's imperious calligraphy. The inspector thought of Ah Q, the absurd and pathetic character Lu Xun had created, a man who believed everything he was told. A thought came into his head, which he banished. No, Anming was *not* like Ah Q . . .

Building Twelve was down an alleyway, a lot less smart than the blocks right by the park, but still no doubt expensive. An entryphone had been installed; there was a lift; the stairs had carpet on them—until the third floor, anyway.

Mrs. Ping was waiting at the door. She was small and flat-faced—a southerner, not even a bit like Xu Yifeng.

"Li's all right?" she asked nervously.

"Of course," said Wang. He tried the old "witness-to-a-serious-crime" routine again, and watched Mrs. Ping's reaction carefully.

"She's not in any danger, is she?"

"None whatsoever," Wang replied.

"Oh, good. Won't you come in?"

"Thank you."

A hall led into a large sitting room. The contents were modern, Western-influenced and not to Wang's taste: pictures in frames, not on proper scrolls; furniture in light wood or metal (Wang's stuff was traditional Chinese and heavy); no books of substance, only ones with pictures in.

"I worry about her, out there in—well, such a remote place, all on her own," said Mrs. Ping.

Wang shook his head. "She's a great deal safer in Shandong than she would be on the streets of a big city."

"Yes. I suppose she is. Can I get you a drink of some kind? Beer? Tea?"

"Professor Xiao says your daughter has an original mind," said the inspector, now ensconced on the sofa, sipping a cup of Five Dragon tea. The Pings had some taste, after all.

Mrs. Ping grinned. "We're terribly proud of her. You know the reputation Fudan has. And to stay on to do postgraduate work . . . We didn't pull any strings, you know."

"No . . ." Wang replied idly.

"She was always bright—as a toddler, at school. D'you want to see some photographs?"

"Yes, please," said Wang. The proud mother went and fetched an album from the bookcase. Wang took it and opened it.

There were no pictures of Ping Li as a small child. The first page showed her in a Young Pioneer's white shirt and red scarf.

Or rather, Xu Yifeng in these clothes.

Wang stared at the picture for what seemed like a lifetime, then glanced up at Mrs. Ping . . .

"I know what you're thinking," she said with a sudden sadness in her voice. Wang was still lost for words.

Mrs. Ping smiled a bitter smile. "Li is not my daughter. Not biologically, though we love her as if she were." She paused. "Ping and I never had children of our own. Little Li was adopted. Back in the bad old days, on Black Dragon River."

19

A vast mechanical roar rammed itself into the inspector's ears. The Shanghai–Jinan sleeper was crossing the Yangzi river.

The bridge—and the river—seemed to go on forever, then the imprisonment was over and silence returned. Bliss, for a moment, till Wang's thoughts went back to the tale he had heard in Mrs. Ping's smart Shanghai flat that evening. It hurt as much to recall as to hear for the first time.

"My husband and I were students in the middle fifties," Mrs. Ping had said. "We were intellectuals and keen Party members. Then Chairman Mao launched that campaign: "let a hundred flowers bloom, let a hundred schools of thought contend"—you won't remember it, Inspector: you're too young. We were to criticize the Party and its leadership; it needed new ideas; anyone who came up with good ones would be rewarded. We thought it was our duty to sit down and do this, the harsher the better—though we were actually very moderate, because we were loyalists. We made our criticisms; we sent them in; we waited for replies. Then the official mood changed. Overnight. Anyone critical of the Party was a rightist. Mao said that five percent of the population were rightists, and insisted that every institution produce lists of them. There were quotas, just like at a factory—five percent of the membership exactly.

"We weren't the most obvious targets, but in the end the numbers had to be made up, and so we found ourselves labelled anyway. Rightists. Enemies of the state. Counter-revolutionaries. We were arrested, questioned, put in a detention centre then shoved into a cattle truck and sent—well, we didn't know where, but we could guess, as it got colder and colder and colder. An Army lorry took us the last part of the journey, through endless pine trees and snow, to a camp with barbed wire, watchtowers, and lines of huts. Naturally, my husband and I were split up: I only caught glimpses of him trudging off in a work party or at meals, queuing up for that revolting gruel we got every day.

"Our work was logging. Cutting down the trees, lopping off branches, sawing up the trunks. Your brain slows down in that kind of cold: people got sent up trees to attach ropes and fell off, people got crushed by trees falling in the wrong direction, people fell into the big main saw—though I think most of those were deliberate suicides. Oh, yes, Inspector, there was plenty of that. The regime drove people to it: relentless self-criticism, in small groups, at huge meetings. Anyone who tried to defend themselves, or anyone else, would get picked on, beaten up, starved—you had to re-duce yourself to nothing, to have no thoughts, ideas, dreams, values, anything human. And then the winter came . . . We were supposed to keep working, but it was impossible. One day a whole party just vanished into a blizzard. We didn't find them till the spring, all huddled together, a few hundred yards from the camp gates. So we sat and shivered in those huts, discussing *People's Daily* editorials or making even more self-criticisms. Acknowl-edge your crimes! Acknowledge your faults! Submit to your superiors! Submit to the law!"

Mrs. Ping sighed. "Other camps, I found out later, were worse. Our commandant was not a cruel man: we found out later he'd got into trouble for falling behind on pro-duction quotas. Some of the guards were sadists, women and men; the trusty prisoners were almost all criminals who hated intellectuals. But you learnt to keep out of their way. We survived. Spring brought warmth—and knee-deep mud as the snow melted. Summer brought the mosquitoes. Enormous ones, that bit in a frenzy.'' She rolled up a sleeve, to reveal a series of blotches on her arm. ''You longed for the cold to come and kill them off—till the cold came, of course . . . In fact, the second winter wasn't as bad as the first. The weakest ones had died already, so there wasn't that perpetual presence of death. And we'd learnt survival skills—physical and mental. And I guess we'd forgotten more about our past lives and didn't care so much. We'd mastered the art of living one day at a time.

''Years passed. You lose count. The food got worse during the great famine, but we still ate. The winter of 'sixty-two was terrible—but we couldn't work in those conditions, so we got through that. Then one day a small group of us, including me and my husband, were summoned to the commandant's office. We expected some petty punishment—but he told us we were free. No reason, no lead-up. We couldn't believe it! Then he added that there was no money for us to go back to our homes, and that there would be no accommodation or work for us when we got there— but if we wanted to stay on, we could move into smaller huts with better heating, eat proper food and get paid a few yuan a week. I'm not sure we actually had a choice, but we pretended we did, then said that we'd decided to stay.'' Mrs. Ping smiled. ''You must think we were crazy, but we were right. A few years later, the Cultural Revolution started and a whole new load of political prisoners arrived. A lot of them were old so-called rightists, coming back for a second stretch. We'd have been among them, but instead we had our huts, our food, a little freedom and some money. So many of the 'sixty-six, 'sixty-seven, 'sixty-eight newcomers just gave up hope and died their first winter . . .

''I don't know when Li's mother came. I do know she was very beautiful. The commandant saw her on parade one day, and simply ordered her out of line and into his office, where he made her a simple offer. I suppose you think she should have been all noble and refused—but you

don't know what it was like out there. I didn't blame her
at all. He treated her well, too. The other new arrivals hated
her, of course, but half of them were soon dead anyway,
so what did it matter? *Aiya*, that sounds so cynical, but I'm
afraid I used up my supply of idealism after about three
weeks in Heilongjiang . . . Sometime later, 'sixty-nine, I
think, a group of Red Guards came and called a meeting
where they criticized the commandant. I'm not sure why—
maybe it was about that business with the quotas. Or maybe
someone just had a grudge against him. It certainly wasn't
for keeping a mistress. He was a broken man after that,
Yifeng said. A few days later, another group arrived and
turned him out of his hut. They arranged for a group of
prisoners to be passing at the same time. Those fellows
literally tore the poor man to pieces.

"Yifeng escaped and hid in our hut. She was pregnant;
she said she wasn't afraid of dying but she wanted the baby
to survive. We said we couldn't protect her—but something
inside me rebelled at this. Maybe I secretly knew what
camp life had done to my own insides . . . I said we should
look after her till the baby was born: she could stay in the
hut; we'd lie to the new commandant and say she was one
of us, and spread the rumour among the other prisoners—
people we looked down on anyway—that she was dead."
Mrs. Ping smiled. "The plan worked. Nobody bothered us,
perhaps because we were paid manual labourers, perhaps
because the prisoners who'd killed the commandant then
went on the rampage and destroyed a whole lot of records.
Yifeng had her little girl.

"Of course, it had to come to light in the end. She only
went out to get air and exercise at night; one of the Cultural
Revolution prisoners spotted her and told the authorities,
no doubt for an extra bread roll or the chance to write a
letter home. Next morning a couple of Red Guards came
round and searched all the 'free' workers' huts. We managed to hide her, but we knew they'd be back, in force. We
had all grown fond of Yifeng by then, so we cooked up
some plan for her to run away. We even pooled our savings.
But she said no, we should keep our money or spend it on

her daughter. She was going to leave on her own, and come back for the baby when she could. We said she'd never get anywhere without help; she insisted. She just got up and walked out into the snow.

"I followed her. She knew the way south towards Harbin, but she headed in the other direction, straight for the Black Dragon River. When she reached the bank, she kept going. It was spring: there was ice, but it was beginning to thaw. The water beneath it was still unspeakably cold, of course, though. I tried to call out to her, but couldn't attract her attention—so I just stood there, watching and listening. Listening was the worst. I can still remember the sound of the ice creaking, then a noise like a gunshot as it shattered, then a kind of muffled splash as Yifeng vanished under it. She never uttered a sound, just sank from view like a statue."

The Shanghai–Jinan sleeper blew its whistle. The noise was inexpressibly mournful, as lonely as a young woman a thousand kilometres from home, in a hell that Yama himself could not have devised. Wang got up and hurried to the toilet, where he bashed the walls in shame and fury.

"I can't remember when I've felt this good," said Wang Anming.

"That's great," Rosina replied.

"You know what they say—'we must make Western things serve China.' And it's all so simple. Just admitting the truth!"

"It's not that simple," Rosina replied. "This is just the start of a long process."

"Ah, but what a start!" He grinned. "I've made some more *jiaozi*. Did you like the last lot?"

"Yes."

"You're not just being nice?"

"No."

"I thought I could go into business making them. When I get that money for my fields, I can buy some equipment, maybe even take on an assistant. I've even thought of a name. The Hundred Flavours Dumpling Company. We could have a slogan: 'let a hundred flavours bloom, let a hundred brands of dumpling contend'!''

Rosina took one of Anming's hundred flavours, dipped it in vinegar and ate it. It was good, no doubt about it.

''So you're abandoning your opposition to the fish-farm, then?'' she asked.

''My new project needs money. And I don't like the sort of people muscling in on the protest group.''

''Fei Baoren will miss you.''

Anming blushed. ''I'm sure she'll be able to . . . I don't know her that well.''

''She greatly admired the way you stood up for her.''

Another blush. ''It was a matter of principle.''

''She respects principle. You should stay in touch with her.''

''Yes. I suppose so.'' He shook his head. ''Her father is such a problem . . .''

''You're forty-four years old!''

''He's one of the bitterest men I've ever met. That's what I mean when I talk about the carrying-pole. History's personal, as well as national.''

Rosina looked pensive. ''Perhaps I ought to try some of my Western psychology on him.''

''Yes,'' said Anming eagerly. ''The poor old sod deserves a bit of tranquillity in his last years.'' He speared a dumpling on a chopstick and offered it to his guest. ''This one's my own special recipe. Dragon's Tail, I call it.''

She took and ate. Delicious.

A bus took Wang from the station at Jinan to Wentai, then he hitched lifts back to Nanping. The driver of the last vehicle, which took him most of the way, was a morose fellow who said three words in their forty shared kilometres. This suited the inspector fine, as his thoughts were on other things.

After hearing Mrs. Ping's story, Wang had been shown Li's room—which was full of traditional scroll paintings. Mrs. Ping had explained how Li's natural mother had been very fond of art, and how the daughter, knowing this from journals her mother had left her, had developed an interest in this too. Mrs. Ping had said she had resented this at first but had learnt to live with it: like most survivors of camps, she knew to accept fate and to make the best of what it gives. Wang had asked, as casually as possible, where the journals were: Mrs. Ping had replied that Li had taken them with her. He had asked her if she had read them, and she had replied: "Only extracts. They're very detailed—and very depressing. Whose house got raided by the Red Guards, what got stolen or destroyed, who got beaten up or put in the cowshed . . ." Mrs. Ping had shaken her head sadly. "Li takes them with her everywhere. It's not healthy—but what can I do?"

"Nothing," Wang had replied.

The lorry pulled up, as requested, at the police station, where Wang got off and went to check if there was any message about the samples that he'd sent off for analysis. There wasn't. He also asked for a copy of the charges against Ma Kai, which Constable Kong typed out for him with his usual slowness. Then, on his way back to the guesthouse, Wang made a diversion to the old cowshed.

The lock had been repaired, but only took a minute or two to pick. Wang removed his jacket, got down on to the floor, began to wriggle under the maize-racks again . . . The hideout was exactly where he'd expected. It even contained the rat-like Mr. Chu's piece of stolen calligraphy. None of Secretary Wu's stuff, of course—not that that would prove anything to Station Chief Huang, who would just assume Ma Kai had hidden that haul somewhere else.

Rosina was out, probably talking to Anming again. Wang was glad for once; he needed to be alone. He spent a long time staring out into space, imagining lines of men and women trudging through snow. Men and women who had done nothing wrong, just made up a quota, a meaningless figure that had sprung from the mind of one man. One man . . . Only when the last line of prisoners had gone could he turn his thoughts to the work in hand.

The murder. He asked himself the main questions of the

case yet again. Who had the Secretary been expecting that evening? Someone whose impending arrival had cheered him up, but who actually turned out to be his killer? If so, who? What role did the paintings play in the affair? Just a blind, or more? Had they once belonged to the Xu family? Was it just coincidence that Xu Yifeng's daughter had appeared in Nanping a few months before the Secretary's death? As was his practice, Wang fetched a notepad and pencil, and began drawing diagrams. In the middle, Secretary Wu; around him, suspects, facts, times, dates, links . . . The wastebin by his side soon filled up; finally he was left with a number of diagrams, several of which (though not all) now led to Ping Li.

Wang put down his work and looked out of the window. It was afternoon. Had he really been working all that time? Yes, and there was nothing new in that. When a case was getting closer to its solution . . . It was, he reflected, too late to act today. He felt glad: he didn't want to act at all.

Revolutionary heroes will never perish.

Wang stood reading the inscription by the fast-fading light. He thought of his own military service, and of his comrades who had fallen in battle, some at his side. The ultimate sacrifice. Then he imagined those prisoners again and heard the tramp of their boots, then the sound of one woman's feet walking out on to ice, then the rending and heaving noises that ice makes under pressure: a warning— go back to the land! Death lies inches beneath your feet! He took out a cheap local cigarette and lit it with a match that blazed like a flare; he smoked urgently and needily, like a suckling child. Xu Yifeng had sacrificed, too. For another person, not an abstraction.

"If the girl killed Secretary Wu, then she must be punished for it," Wang told himself. He repeated the sentence a few times, to see if it degenerated into nonsense, the way slogans do. It didn't, though it didn't uplift him the way great truths did, either. It was what you had to believe to be a good policeman. It was enough.

He finished the vile cigarette and stubbed it out on the concrete.

20

Station Chief Huang was happy to lend Wang one of his motorbikes next morning. The criminal Ma Kai was on the edge of cracking; if he did so while the Beijing policeman was elsewhere in the province, so much the better. It would just underline how much he, Huang Guo, had solved this case on his own.

Rosina was less happy about Wang's trip: a twenty-five-year-old lookalike of Xu Yifeng was waiting at the other end, and who knew what tricks such a woman might try if cornered? So she had been particularly affectionate in bed last night; her husband had looked genuinely regretful as he set off that morning—but the worry remained. Best do something, something a bit challenging, to take her mind off things. First stop, the clinic, and Fei Baoren . . .

The inspector's mood was mixed. The bike felt good, and made light work of the dirt roads. The task at the other end . . . had to be done.

The bike bumped its way up the main street of Wushui village and came to a stop outside Party HQ. This place was poor, the surrounding countryside barren and dry, the buildings wooden shacks or crumbling brick hovels. The

clothes of the children who gathered to watch the rider
dismount and knock on the metal front door of Wushui's
one proper building would have disgraced Nanping's old
village . . .

"Come in, Comrade Wang," said an old lady in a Mao
suit. "We got your message. I'm afraid Secretary Fang is
out in his fields today, but I can take you down to see the
student . . ."

". . . We can't understand why she wants to come here,"
said the lady (who had turned out to be Secretary Fang's
mother) as they walked down the rutted street, followed by
a small snake of ragamuffins.

"Research, isn't it?"

"There's not much to research here."

"She's an economist."

"*Aiya*, that's all about money, isn't it? Perhaps you'd
better tell her she's come to the wrong place: we haven't
got any. Here's the house."

Wang noted with interest that a moped was parked down
the side. He wouldn't have liked to have ridden such a
vehicle across dirt roads by night, but it was certainly possible to do so . . . He knocked on the door.

"Hello," said a voice with a Shanghai accent. "Who is
it?"

"Someone to see you," said Mrs. Fang, "from—where
was it?"

"Police," said Wang.

There was a long pause, then the door opened.

Despite the photographs, the sight of Xu Yifeng's daughter came as a shock. Wang was lost for words again.

"You'd better come in," said the ghost.

Mrs. Fang looked disappointed that she wasn't going to
see any more of this encounter—as did the kids, who had
now formed themselves into a semi-circle—but Wang
thanked her and followed Ping Li into her temporary home.

The young student lived, as the local people probably
almost all did, in one room. There was a desk, two chairs,
a table, a stove, an old-fashioned *kang* bed. On the wall
was one scroll, with a classical landscape on it.

"Is everything all right?" said Ping Li, once the door was shut. "Nothing's happened to my parents, has it?"

"No."

"Good. Sit down. Sorry about the mess. What's the problem?"

"I'm from Nanping," said Wang.

Ping Li's relaxed expression was gone. "What's been happening there?"

Wang showed her his ID. "Name sound familiar?"

"Ah." She appeared to relax. "You're Wang Anming's brother."

"I am. He's still drinking, you know."

"I'm sorry to hear that."

"Are you?"

Ping Li smiled. "Ah. So you know the story, then?"

"Yes. Your mother's death, the journal she left you."

"Then you should understand how I feel."

"I do, in a way. Your mother was an honourable woman."

Ping Li looked at him carefully. "That's what I think," she said after a while. "I'm surprised at an employee of the Public Security Bureau thinking so, too."

"Life is full of surprises," Wang said with a smile.

Ping Li, who had clearly learnt to distrust smiling policemen, increased her look of suspicion. "Why are you here, then?"

"To ask questions. Tell me who else you 'haunted.' "

The young student seemed happy to reel off some names.

"Not Teacher Zhang?" said Wang at the end. "Surely, as his uncle was the Red Guards' leader . . ."

"There were enough people who'd actually done things, without having to go down the generations. I know that's not very Chinese—Chairman Mao didn't feel avenged until an enemy's whole family was punished. But I don't want to be like Chairman Mao."

"And Chu Youming? A farmer. Face like a rat . . ."

Ping Li's face fell. "Oh, yes. Him. I didn't bother much with him. No reason to." She had gone red.

"And Secretary Wu?"

She hardly reacted at all. "Well, naturally I visited the Party Secretary. And he didn't even recognize me. So there wasn't a lot of point in being the ghost of Xu Yifeng with him." She shook her head. "I don't think he had much to do with my family's suffering, anyway. Yes, he had power during the Cultural Revolution, but it was all exercised from behind a desk. Some folk resent even that—but I wanted the ones who went out and caused the damage."

"He also used the Cultural Revolution to build up his art collection," Wang said gently. "Albeit indirectly . . ."

"No doubt," came Ping Li's casual reply. "He had some nice stuff."

"Stuff which had originally belonged to your family?"

"Oh, no." She shook her head. "You're right; I hoped he would have. But he didn't. Nobody did: I'm afraid Red Tiger Zhang and Chairman Mao and your brother made as good a job of destroying our family property as they did of destroying my family."

Wang winced, but wasn't going to be put off. "I think that Secretary Wu had eight pieces from your family collection."

"No! He didn't have any. Mother described every item in her journal, in great detail. Wu didn't have one."

"Did Farmer Chu?"

Ping Li shook her head uneasily—and reddened again. She was not a good liar. And thus, probably, not a killer. Wang thought back to his deliberations of last night, and felt a wave of relief. But he still had work to do.

"Tell me about Ma Kai."

This time Ping Li's reaction was violent. Wide eyes, a gasp, headshakes. "I don't know who you're talking about . . ."

"He's confessed to the robberies," Wang said.

"W-what robberies?"

All Wang did was stay silent and fix her with a stare.

"Tell me how you met him," he said finally.

More silence. One of an interrogator's best tools.

"It was at the snooker hall. I was sitting in my room at Yang's one evening, reading some academic study on—I can't remember—when I realized I was bored. So I put on the one sexy outfit I'd brought with me, and walked round the village till I found somewhere interesting. I walked in; all the boys stared at me; Kai had the guts to come over and get talking. And he wasn't just a talker, either . . . You look shocked, Old Wang. Students are boring; campus life is boring; it's not nineteen eighty-eight any longer. Our homegrown repression and all this political correctness that's so fashionable in the West have seen to that. I went all the way with Ma Kai, and I thoroughly enjoyed it!''

Wang, a lot less shocked than he apparently looked, simply said: "And you planned the robberies with him?"

"*No*! Has he been telling you that?"

"I haven't talked to him."

"So—how come you knew about him and me?"

"I worked it out. That's my job. Tell me what role you had in the robberies.''

"And then you'll arrest me?"

"No."

Ping Li's puzzlement looked genuine. "I had no role. Apart from recommending Farmer Chu as a target.''

"Just that?"

"Yes."

"You're lying again."

"OK, I asked him to steal that calligraphy. It *had* been ours. It was the only piece I found in the whole village. Isn't it a crime to receive stolen goods? That's what Chu had done, via Tiger Zhang and that little runt of a man, Ting. *Ai*, there's someone I'd like to have haunted! But Ting was dead, of course.''

"Tell me about your visit to Secretary Wu."

More puzzlement. "It was boring. We sat and talked about what we were supposed to talk about: politics, history, economics—for a man with no formal training, he had a reasonable grasp of the subject.''

"This was at his house?"

"Yes. Nice place."

"He wasn't in the habit of letting strangers in."

"I'd heard that. So I wore my snooker-hall outfit when

I went to see him in his office to ask for a proper interview. Then a terrible old Mao jacket and trousers when I actually did go and see him.'' She smiled. ''I think he was disappointed, but he did his duty and went on with the interview anyway. I suppose as a man, you disapprove.''

Wang grinned evasively. ''Tell me about Wu's pictures.''

''There's nothing to tell. They weren't ours, that's all I know.''

Ping Li's face reddened. If they *were* hers . . . But the lie was probably in the second part of the sentence.

''Someone stole them,'' said Wang.

''Oh. It wasn't me. Or Kai.''

''But you know who it might have been.''

''No. Why should I?''

''Shall we try 'because Secretary Wu was killed by the thief, and because Ma Kai currently stands accused of the killing, and will soon have a false confession beaten out of him by the local police if I don't find out who really did do the murder?' ''

Ping Li said nothing for a long time. Then, ''You're lying.''

''Why should I do that?''

''Because you're a policeman. What d'you really want?''

''The truth. And for Ma Kai not to be executed for a crime he didn't commit.''

''What's that to you?''

''Injustice?''

''Pfah! You're a policeman!'' Li glared at him defiantly, then looked away and fell silent. Wang let her stay that way, reflecting as he did so on the sad state of relations between intelligent young folk and the forces of law and government. Then he thought of the end this woman's mother had met . . . He took out the list of charges against Ma Kai and gave it to her.

''If you don't tell me the whole truth, that young man will die. Like an animal, grovelling on his knees, with his hands behind his back. His family will even get sent a bill for the bullet.''

Ping Li stared at the list for a long time. Then she began to cry. Then she said, not to Wang but to the room, to someone in her own mind, "Forgive me." Then, conquering her sobs, she told Wang, "He was so good to my mother. They were in the cowshed together; he'd do extra work for her, give her food, everything. His own wife had died, you see . . ." She glanced up at the policeman with the beseeching look of a child. "They were *his* family's paintings. And I told him about them. That smug bastard Wu had had them all those years, and he hadn't even known . . ."

"How did you know they were his?" Wang asked slowly. He felt oddly untriumphant, despite the fact he now knew the killer's identity.

"The journals. My mother described several collections, not just ours. She knew what would happen to them; she hoped someone like me would come along and restore justice later. Instead . . ."

The young orphan began to cry again. Wang thought of Rosina, then reached out a hand to her, the hand of compassion.

21

"So you're ready to confess, Ma Kai?"

"Yes."

"Good. I knew you'd see sense." Station Chief Huang looked across the desk at the young prisoner and allowed himself a smile. "You'll be amazed how much better you feel when you've told us everything."

"So I can die happy?"

"That's not my decision. I can only control the way your family are treated. Now, tell me the story."

"I don't know it."

"Don't play games. Not now you've made your mind up. You planned a raid on Secretary Wu's house."

"Yes. I knew he was rich. Party bosses all are. So I went there and broke in."

"How?"

"I can't remember."

"Try. A side window? In the kitchen?"

"That's right. A side window. In the kitchen. And I found the house full of CD players, videos—"

"Secretary Wu collected paintings."

"And paintings. Lots of them. Calligraphy, too?"

"Calligraphy, too. Then?"

"Then—I was looking round the living room, when I heard a noise. From upstairs—it does have two storeys, the house I burgled, doesn't it?"

"You know bloody well it does."

"Well, the old bugger was asleep. And there was me, convinced he'd gone out. All the other robberies, I made sure the owner wasn't about. This one—well, I guess I got over-confident. Anyway, he woke up. And came down the stairs to investigate. I—what did I do?—I tried to hide. Behind a sofa? Yes. And he came into the room. Of course, his paintings were missing. And his calligraphy. So he realized he'd been burgled. He says: 'I know you're still here. I'm going to kill you.' So he takes a gun out of his pocket, and begins prowling round, looking in all the corners. Finally, of course, the sofa is the last place left. He walks up to it, he holds out the gun with one hand; with the other, he pulls the sofa away from the wall . . . Then I wake up."

"Stop fucking about, Ma Kai. You hit him."

"Yes, I hit him. With . . ."

"A heavy blunt object."

"What heavy blunt object?"

"Er—a piece of wood."

"A piece of wood. On the head?"

Huang nodded.

"How many blows, Chief?"

"You know, Ma. This bullshit won't do you any good."

"I rain blows down on him. I'm terrified. Then I suddenly realize I've killed him. I panic, and run away—taking the paintings, even though I know I won't be able to sell them."

Huang finished writing. "Sign this. It may save your life."

"It'll certainly save your job."

The chief called out for Constable Kong. "Take this piece of shit away from here," he said.

By the time he got back to Nanping, Wang had the story clearly worked out in his mind. He crossed Snake Pass, paused where the path led off to the guesthouse, then carried on into the village. No point in wasting time.

He rode into the courtyard of the police station, parked by the door and walked in. Station Chief Huang was in his office. And looking very happy.

"I've done it!" the chief announced.

"What?"

"Got that little fucker to confess." He handed over a typewritten sheet, signed "Ma Kai." "Go on, Wang, read it."

Wang took it and read. For a moment, his hand was unsteady—then a broad smile crossed his face. "It's false," he said.

"False? What d'you mean, false? He's signed it. He dictated it to me half an hour ago!"

"What about the office light?"

"Bugger the office light. It says there, he killed the Secretary."

"The light was on. Any thief would notice that. It's easy to check if the room is occupied . . . And what's this about "striking the Secretary with a piece of wood?' "

"It's a confession, damn you, Wang. You think you're so bloody clever; you tell me what really happened."

The inspector did so.

At the end of it all, Station Chief Huang shook his head. "You don't seem to have much proof," he said in a dull voice. "It's just a story. An interesting story, but nothing more. For example, that girl might have been lying. She's an intellectual; people like that aren't reliable."

"Will you come with me and check it? After all, you've done all you can with Ma Kai."

"And more!"

"If you come, and if my story's true, it'll look good for you," said Wang. "I don't want any credit."

The chief looked thoughtful, then said: "OK."

Station Chief Huang led the way to the murderer's house, down a long muddy path that led at first between high walls then out across fields. They crossed a stream and walked up a stone-flagged path. He rapped imperiously on the door;

Wang put his finger to his lips and said: "Gently."

A voice from inside asked who it was.

"Wang Anzhuang," Wang replied.

"Ah." The door opened. Wang hadn't seen Fei Zhaoling before; he only had descriptions from Rosina and, more recently, Ping Li. But this individual seemed to fit. "Fei Zhaoling?" he asked, anyway. The man nodded.

"You're under arrest!" The voice was the chief's, who had pressed himself against the wall out of sight, but who had now bounded into view. The door slammed shut in an instant.

"You bloody fool!" Wang exclaimed.

"You said he was a murder suspect. Therefore it is my responsibility to arrest him."

"Let him answer the questions first!"

"He can do that at the station. Anyway, he's refused arrest, which is a crime in itself. I'm going in to get him."

"No. That's totally the wrong—" Wang began, but the chief was already hammering at the lock with his boot. "*Stop!*"

Huang kept on kicking. Wang grabbed him and pulled him away: the chief rounded on his fellow policeman and made as if to hit him. Then he stopped, in mid-blow, shrank back and gave a very foolish grin.

"Sorry. All that work I put in on Ma Kai . . ."

"Help me over the wall," said the inspector. "Then watch round the back to see if he tries to run."

The chief meekly formed his hands into a stirrup; Wang pulled himself up on to the big wall that surrounded the Fei courtyard.

"Watch the back," the inspector reminded his colleague, and was gone.

Wang dropped down into the front passage of the yard. He knew the layout, because almost all courtyard homes in China followed it: a dog-leg corridor from the front door into the quadrangle, accommodation round the three other sides of the square (traditionally the north, east and west sides). He also knew it would be best to act swiftly: he hadn't wanted it to be this way, but it was; he had to catch

Fei Zhaoling while the fellow was still confused. Wang paused just briefly for one deep *qigong* breath, then ran round the corner into the quad. The sight that greeted him filled him with horror.

Fei Zhaoling had a gun. An old Browning. And he was holding it to the head of a hostage. A female hostage. Rosina.

Wang froze. "How the . . . ?" he mumbled.

Fei Zhaoling smiled. "You weren't expecting this, were you, Comrade Gold-badge?"

Wang was still lost for words.

"Your good wife came round to talk to me, to offer me some kind of help for my—what was it you called it?" Fei Zhaoling had a hand across Rosina's mouth, so clearly wasn't too concerned about an answer.

"Let her go," said Wang.

"Why?"

"She's nothing to do with this."

"She's everything to do with this. She's your wife. And she's a Party member, like you. This is all to do with the Party, and what it does to innocent people."

"It's all to do with the past. Rosina has no role in your past."

Fei Zhaoling laughed. "She has a key role in my present."

Rosina tried to wriggle free, and her captor tightened his grip. Wang fought back the impulse to attack: the old man had the gun.

Think back to your training. Rule One: keep them talking.

"What d'you want?"

"Freedom. A passage to Taiwan. But your people won't keep their promises, will they?"

No. But don't tell him that.

"No," Fei Zhaoling went on, "I can see from your face that they won't. So I guess it's just death on my own terms. Which means taking two Party members with me."

Wang thought fast. "I keep *my* promises," he said.

"What do you mean by that?"

"I mean that none of this absurd scene ever happened—"

"Your pal Huang is probably staring at us now through the windows."

"He hasn't got the intelligence. Let her go!"

Rosina gave a muffled cry. She was trying to say something, over and over again. Two syllables—

Of course! "Think of your daughter," said Wang. "Think what Baoren will go through if you kill us."

Fei Zhaoling pondered, then spoke. "You already think I'm a murderer, of a Party official. Poor little Baoren will suffer anyway. As she always has. *Aiya*, you Party bastards don't give a fart one way or the other about her."

"That's not true. Why do you think my wife came round to talk to you?"

"To spy on me?"

"I'm not that stupid. D'you think I'd send in a spy then turn up the way Huang and I did? Let her go, and let's talk sensibly. For Baoren's sake."

Fei Zhaoling began shaking his head. Then he glanced across to the east-side room, to the bright curtains his daughter had put up there. Rosina felt the grip around her head tighten, then loosen, more and more and—

She broke free, and ran across to her husband, who held his arms wide apart, both to embrace her and to show Fei Zhaoling he wasn't going for a weapon. The gunman watched this scene with cold disapproval, then waggled the Browning to remind the participants who was in charge.

"Sit down. And apart. A metre apart."

Wang and Rosina did so.

"Put your hands out in front of you. Good." Fei Zhaoling glanced from the gun to his two captives and back again. A look of pleasure crossed his face. "Your father labelled me a rich peasant," he said at length. "He took my land away, forced me to work like a slave on fields my family had owned, set spies on me day and night."

"He protected you," Wang replied. "Other cadres would have called your family landlords and looked the other way while a mob came killing and looting."

"That came later."

"In the Cultural Revolution? My father was dead by then. He would never have allowed that."

"He was still my first persecutor. And it was his Party, his leader, who launched the Cultural Revolution. D'you know what it was like?"

Rule One. "Tell me," said Wang.

The former "rich peasant" glanced down at his gun again. "I shall. Imagine this place, twenty-eight years ago, when I was a young man, Baoren a little girl and her grandfather Yeye still alive. It's evening; there's been a big meeting in North Square, at which our 'case' was to be discussed. We know what's going to happen, and sure enough, it does. We hear voices, shouting slogans that I can still remember now. Long live Chairman Mao! Long live the Great Proletarian Cultural Revolution! Death to all Capitalist Roaders! Soon they're all round us; they want us to 'come out and answer for our crimes'; they say they have cans of petrol and will set light to us. And they stop the political slogans; it's just 'Kill! Kill! Kill!' How d'you think that feels?"

As an ex-soldier, Wang had a good idea how it felt, but he reckoned a shake of the head would be more encouraging to the speaker.

It was. "It was Yeye who saved us. He told us to gather up all the paintings in the house, and to run out with them. Imagine him and me and even little Baoren, ripping our beloved collection off the wall and running across this yard with it in our arms . . . Then we open the door, the selfsame door I opened a few minutes ago to you and that pig Huang: this time it's a huge crowd of Huangs, all full of mindless hate. Have you ever seen a hundred people wanting to kill you? It's an unforgettable experience."

Another shake of the head.

"Yeye tried to offer the paintings to the leader of the mob," Fei Zhaoling went on. "He'd heard that Party boss Kang Sheng collected art; maybe Tiger Zhang did too, or would want to seek favour with Kang. Instead, they just ordered us to build a bonfire." The old man closed his eyes for a moment, as the pain of the memory was too much.

For a second, Wang contemplated action—but Fei Zhaoling opened his eyes again and gave the Browning a reassuring pat. "I expect you think it's sentimental to love art. Bourgeois, reactionary, decadent and so on. Maybe it is, but I loved those paintings. I grew up with them; I lived in them in my imagination. I dreamt that when I met the woman I truly loved—not my wife, I'm afraid, that was an arranged thing—it would be on the bank of a sunlit river.

"Tiger Zhang said our pictures were all old culture and fit only to be burned. He was just about to douse them in petrol, when one of his sidekicks came up and tried to save them, as Yeye had hoped. Zhang let him take a few away—eight, I suppose, for that was the number that Secretary Wu had in his house. The rest he put to the torch. Whoosh! A family's pride all gone up in useless smoke.

"That was just the beginning, of course. We were paraded down the main street in dunce's caps a few weeks later, then made to stand on a public stage bent forward with our arms straight and tied together behind our backs—a jet-plane ride, that was called. Have you any idea how much that hurts? In your forearms, in your shoulders, all down your back? Old Yeye never stood properly again. And then we were packed off to the cowshed, us and two other local families and various farm animals. We lived like the animals; we were worked like the animals; we ate like them, slept like them and we died like them. Oh yes, died like them. Old Xu and his son were just taken out one evening and slaughtered. For no reason. And Xu Yifeng was sent away to die."

Fei Zhaoling shook his head. "I wanted to meet her by a river and share my life with her; instead I met her in a cowshed and she was taken away to a river to die alone. Murdered, by the Communist Party of China . . . I vowed revenge, though I wasn't sure how, or when, or even on whom. And I never quite forgot that vow, even though I came to think it impractical—Baoren depended on me, you see."

"She still does," said Wang.

"Worse luck for her."

Silence fell. The inspector broke it. "Tell me the rest of the story."

"What rest?"

"You know 'what rest.' "

Fei Zhaoling glanced at his gun again and carried on. "Of course, the Cultural Revolution ended. 1976, I think it was. And things got a little bit better. But not that much. They never really took the class hats off. Secretary Wu, Deputy Yao and his wife, your Station Chief Huang—they never let us forget our background. We got land rights back; Baoren got the job she wanted; everybody had a bit more money. But the stigma remained. In nineteen eighty-six, Baoren met a doctor and they wanted to get married. Mrs. Yao stopped it: the village had quotas for marriage, and they were all full. With poor-peasant categories. I couldn't get a job at Wei's factory: Public Security gave me a bad reference. Then Wu came up with this fish-farm scheme. Those fields were all I had to live off; the money would have vanished in no time, with inflation, with taxes. Then along came Ping Li . . ."

Fei Zhaoling winced as if with physical pain. "I chased her away the first time. I thought she really was a ghost. Then she wrote me a note, and I realized the truth. It was like having a second daughter! And she told me what fun she'd been having, haunting her family's old tormentors. We roared with laughter at some of her stories. Good loyal Red Guards lying, giggling, squirming with embarrassment, blushing, turning pale with fear . . . She also said how she'd been searching for her family art collection at the same time, but had had very little luck. But with mine, which her mother had described in her journal, she'd done better. Eight pieces, all on the walls of the same luxury villa. And then she said which luxury villa . . .

"First I had to see them for myself. That wasn't easy. I tried spying on the Secretary one night, but you can't really see into his front room. Not unless you walk right up to the window, and I didn't fancy that: lights might have gone on, alarm bells, anything. And anyway, I had a better idea.

I'd be like Ping Li; I'd lie my way into the house itself. So I did. I said . . .'' His voice faltered.

"You'd betray the ecology group?" Wang suggested.

Fei Zhaoling looked ashamed. "I had no intention of doing so, of course. So why not say that? We had to meet to discuss details, and I couldn't be seen entering Party HQ for the first time in my life, could I? Wu fell for it completely. I made my way up to that bloody villa—there was no one else on the road, apart from Teacher Zhang and a couple of rich merchants, and I just hid from them. I found the place and rang the bell. Secretary Wu, the man who'd organized my persecution for decades, answered the door with a big smile and a string of platitudes about progress and forgetting the past and so on. Then he showed me into his sitting room.

"There they were. After twenty-six years. The Jiaqing calligraphy; the boats on the river. My river! And the man who'd effectively stolen them from me—in the name of equality—sat me down in a chair more comfortable than anything I've ever sat in, got me tea in a Jingdezhen cup, offered me a pitiful bribe to betray everything I stood for, and started blabbing on about his bloody fish-farm . . . Then he asked me what I was looking at, and I told him. And he lied straight back; the pictures had belonged to his grandfather.

"It was that that did it. That lie, and the way he told it: if I say so, it's true, because of who I am. Party Secretary Wu Changyan. And at the same moment I saw Karl Marx, the grand originator of all the lying and the stealing and the killing, up on a shelf, looking down at me with that smug expression. Wu had some form he wanted me to sign; he'd bent down to pick it up . . .''

Fei Zhaoling clenched his fists and face muscles. "I never thought I could kill anybody. But it was easy." He reddened. "In fact, I enjoyed it. It was my revenge, the revenge I'd promised myself but almost forgotten about: for Xu Yifeng, for my river, for our family home. And for Baoren's marriage, for those jet-plane rides, for the cow-shed, for the prejudice—for thirty years of humiliation and lies.'' He shook his head. "Those lies! First you try and fight them, then you try and put up with them, then suddenly they're inside you, and you're beginning to live them. Then I picked up Karl Marx—thump!—and I was free.'' He gave a gesture of happy abandon with his non-gun hand. "Free! You probably don't even know what the word means, comrades.''

Wang was wrestling with some definition based on law and justice, when Rosina spoke up. "I know very well what freedom means. It's something you lost the moment you killed that old man.''

Fei Zhaoling rounded on her with a look of fury. Wang's spirits fell. This is what he'd meant about letting amateurs get involved in police matters. "Rosina—'' he began.

"I mean exactly what I say,'' she cut in. "If you'd really been free, you would have told Secretary Wu to go to hell with his deal and his paintings and his fish-farm and everything else. Instead, you played his game, his way. You won that little skirmish—but the Party's won the war.''

"What d'you mean?'' Fei Zhaoling snapped.

"The Party obtained power by violence. It retains power by violence. After years of passive resistance, you joined in that violence. You agreed to play things their way. Who said: 'Political power grows out of the barrel of a gun'?''

"Chairman Mao.''

"And what are you waving at us?''

Fei Zhaoling said nothing.

"There is a proper way out of this ridiculous situation,'' Rosina went on. "A way out that gives you your freedom back, that shows you're better than Secretary Wu and the Yaos and Station Chief Huang. And Chairman Mao. Put that gun down, accept that what you did to Secretary Wu was wrong, look into your own heart and—''

Fei Zhaoling steeled himself. "Pfah! That's woman's talk. Soft, sentimental—''

"I work with the sick and dying,'' Rosina replied calmly. "You can't be soft or sentimental there. And there's no room for lies—the Party's or anyone else's. D'you know what the biggest lie of all is?''

Fei Zhaoling, in spite of himself, shook his head.

"It's simple," Rosina went on. "It's that human life doesn't matter, that killing can be justified by clever words. Karl Marx's clever words, Chairman Mao's clever words, Red Tiger Zhang's clever words. And now, since you found this illusory 'freedom' by killing an old man, Fei Zhaoling's clever words. 'It's OK to kill because of what happened in the past, because of history.' That's just what Mao and Marx and Lenin and Stalin and Engels all said. But it isn't OK and it never will be."

Fei Zhaoling's gun hand suffered the slightest of tremors.

"If you really want to beat the Party, you'll put that thing down," Rosina continued. "Use it on us, and you're just playing their game. And all the resistance you've put up, all that you've fought to protect and nurture—your dignity, your daughter's future and reputation—this will all be wasted and destroyed. Two pulls of a trigger and you negate your whole life."

The old rich peasant said nothing for a while, then spoke. "It's a bit late for all that, isn't it?"

"Not while you've got that gun in your hand. It's done you one turn, that thing. It's given you a second chance to be free. Really free."

"Then to die like an animal."

"No. Like a human being. As long as you can choose: honourably or shamefully, having lived by your beliefs or having given in to the Party's."

"How d'you know what I believe?" Fei Zhaoling snapped.

"I know what Baoren believes," Rosina said. "And I know the respect she has for you. Leave her that."

As if on cue, Baoren's colourful curtains billowed in the wind. Something in the world outside—you could see straight through the room—flashed in the sun.

"Put that gun down," Rosina went on, "and I'll tell her how you defeated Marx and Mao and Red Tiger Zhang and the whole Communist Party of China by one simple action. She'll build a memorial to you in her heart that puts that stupid piece of concrete in Snake Valley to shame."

The old peasant's eyes returned to the Browning. Its
black-market purchase had cost every yuan he'd saved, but
he'd felt so good buying it. A freedom fighter. A revolutionary.

"Your daughter loves you," said Rosina.

Political power grows out of the barrel of a gun.

Says Chairman Mao.

"She needs you now, more than ever," said Rosina.

The door of the compound opened. Station Chief Huang,
looking through binoculars, whispered a command to Constable Kong.

"Get ready."

Three figures emerged.

"What's happening?" said Kong.

"You can see as well as I can!" Huang snapped back.
"That woman, Wang's wife, seems to be helping Fei
Zhaoling. Extraordinary. He was threatening them with a
gun—I saw it, through the windows. He's crazy. No change
in orders."

Constable Kong adjusted the focus on the telescopic
sights, with which a Dragunov sniper's rifle is accurate over
several hundred yards.

He only needed one shot.

22

Wang and Rosina lay in bed. It was mid-morning; they seemed to have lost all desire to do anything but hold each other. No sex, just reassurance. Then they heard a noise from the room next door.

"Our neighbour's back!" said Wang.

"So?"

"I must find out what he was doing here. And what he discovered about the Snake Valley ambush."

"Who cares?"

"I must find out."

Wang knocked on the door. The man who opened it was wrinkled and wizened, like those poor-quality oranges from Hainan that used to be the only ones you could get.

"Lian Gang?"

"That's my name. What d'you want?"

"I'm staying next door. My name's Wang Anzhuang."

"Oh," Lian replied.

He clearly wasn't the conversational type, so Wang produced his ID. "I have some questions to ask you."

Lian looked puzzled. "You'd better come in, Inspector."

Wang did so. "I believe you were investigating the his-

tory of the Snake Valley ambush,'' he said, once they had
sat down.

The old man started. "How did you know that?"

"It's my business to know things. But I need to know
more—what you have found out, and who from."

"Who from . . . ? I can't tell you. Why should I? What's
this about?"

"A murder investigation."

"Oh. Who's been murdered?"

"Party Secretary Wu Changyan."

Lian froze. "When?" he asked.

"The Wednesday before last."

"What time?"

"Evening."

"Ah, well, I was on my way to Liaoning province. To
see . . ." He paused, in need of an alibi but unwilling to
reveal any more than he had to. "A man called Han Haotong."

Wang half guessed this was coming, so was able to show
no reaction. "Who's Han Haotong?"

"An old soldier who was in the column that was ambushed."

"How did you find out about him?"

"Research. I retired not long ago, and decided to devote
some time to solving this mystery. I've always been interested in the Civil War. And I like mysteries. No doubt you
do too."

Wang nodded, though he wasn't totally convinced by
Lian's story. "What did he tell you?"

Lian sighed. "Nothing. His granddaughter warned me
that would probably happen, but said if I wanted to try my
luck I was welcome. So I did. But he's totally senile. I
couldn't get a word of sense out of him."

"Shame. That's a long way to go for nothing."

"You have to try."

"I guess you do. And you've no other leads?"

"Not yet. But I've got the rest of my life."

Wang nodded. He knew he should get up and leave now,

but—as usual—he didn't. "Your real name is Shen, isn't it?" he said instead.

Lian looked horrified.

"Shen Zirong was—your brother?" Wang went on. "Yes, I can see he was. I had to do a little research into the ambush, too. All in the line of duty, of course. If it's any consolation to you, I wish you every success in clearing his name. He was obviously innocent of the crimes attributed to him." He paused.

Now go.

Wang stayed. "I owe you an apology, Mr. Shen," he went on. "Or rather my family owes one to your family. My father was Wang Jingfu."

Lian said nothing for a long time.

"My father had no option but to sign that order," Wang added finally.

"That's what they all say," Lian replied.

"Maybe. Some of 'them' mean it." Wang sighed. "So many injustices occurred in the old days. The passage of time doesn't mitigate them: I've learnt that in the last three weeks. Only human forgiveness can do that. That's not easy to give: I've learnt that too. But I ask for it, anyway."

"Go to hell," said the old man.

Later that morning, a call came through from Station Chief Huang (soon, the rumour went, to be Party Secretary Huang, after the policeman's brave action in rescuing the two hostages).

"There's a report here from Beijing. Something to do with writing paper, ink and stuff."

"What does it say?"

"Initial tests reveal the two sheets to come from the same source. As do the ink and the glue. They want to know if further investigation is required."

Wang pondered. Then a wicked smile crossed his face. "Tell them no," he said.

A letter also arrived that morning, from Wang's sister Anchun.

"Look at *that* writing paper," said Rosina. "She'll be using silk next. What does it say?"

" 'I am having the flat redecorated, and have no spare cash at the moment. Try me in a few months' time—though I can't help feeling that throwing money at Anming won't cure his illness. What he needs to do is depend less on handouts and take more responsibility for himself.' "

Rosina shook her head.

"I suppose we can afford something," said Wang.

Rosina walked with ever-increasing trepidation. The fields, the stream, the stone-flagged path. A knock on the door.

One of the neighbours opened it. "She's in her room," she said. "She won't see anyone, but you can try if you like."

Rosina went in, remembering her feelings as she had last left this place. Then the sound of that shot.

"Baoren?" She tapped on the window. How ironic those bright curtains, pulled back and hanging limp, now looked.

A figure in the room turned round. Red-eyed, pale as a ghost. "You!"

"I'm terribly sorry."

"Sorry!"

"Yes. There are things I must tell you."

"There's nothing I want to hear from you." Baoren shook her head. "To think, I trusted you . . ."

"Listen to me!"

"No. Go away!"

"Your father said—"

"Don't mention him. His name, on your lips—it's disgusting. Long Live the Party! Those are your words, Rosina Wang. Death to all Capitalist Roaders! Exterminate all Poisonous Weeds! Learn from the People's Liberation Army! Support—"

"Shut up and listen to what I've got to say!"

"Criticize Confucius and Lin Biao! Seek Truth from Facts! Work to Build the Four Modernizations!"

Rosina began banging her fists on the windowframe. "Stop. Stop! *Stop! Stop!*"

She stopped, and silence had fallen. The ghost had floated out of view. The main door opened. Baoren stood in it. "Come in," she said.

Rosina did as she was asked. They walked through into Baoren's room; Baoren pointed to a chair; Rosina sat down.

"I know how you must feel at the moment," Rosina began, "but I have to tell you what happened. And how I feel about it." She then recounted the story of the siege, with as much accuracy as she could. Baoren sat and listened in silence, except for a huge sob of grief at the end. Drying her eyes, she looked up at Rosina and spoke in a quiet voice.

"Thank you, Rosina. But it's still true that if you and your husband hadn't gone snooping into this business, my father would still be alive. I know, that thief would have been shot, but I'm afraid I don't care about him. I care about my father and me. Our lives have been destroyed."

Rosina bowed her head. "Your life hasn't been destroyed. I'll do all I can to make sure of that."

Baoren looked at her with distrust but said nothing.

Time, that was what she needed. Something Rosina had very little of.

On the way back to the village, Rosina met Station Chief Huang. The chief grinned with pleasure as he saw her coming: he had already convinced himself of his own story, and was looking forward to being greeted as the young Beijinger's saviour.

"Morning, Mrs. Wang! Good to be alive, eh!"

"Yes. Er, where are you going?"

"To the Fei household. There are a lot of questions Miss Fei Baoren has to answer."

"Leave her for a bit, please."

"Leave her? She might abscond. She has charges to answer. Conspiracy to murder, conspiracy to possess and conceal a firearm. You were very fortunate, you know."

"I'm sure she didn't conspire to anything. And I—"

"We'll establish that by official procedures. And there's the business of the stolen paintings to sort out. They belong to Secretary Wu's estate.'' The chief looked at her. ''You don't reform people by being soft on them, you know, Mrs. Wang. Her father nearly killed you. I don't understand your attitude at all.''

Wang finished packing early. ''Let's go for a walk,'' he said, but Rosina shook her head and replied, ''I've still got stuff to sort out. You go.''

''OK.'' Wang was secretly pleased again: he wanted to be alone with his place of birth for a while.

Rosina sat down to write the letters. To Baoren, a simple proposition; to the heroic local policeman a simple request (for clemency) backed with a simple threat (of revelation); to Anming some information about how he would—after a little time—be looked after by the recipient of the first letter.

That great Chinese god, fate, would carry the story on if it chose to.

The inspector's walk took him through the old village, out to the cowshed—Ping Li and Ma Kai, what a strange match, but wasn't it often said how opposites attract? Yin and Yang. Then up the hillside, along a winding path to the view point which he and Rosina still hadn't visited. Past Secretary Wu's villa. On to the track up to Snake Pass, on down into the valley. Finally, the memorial: *Revolutionary heroes will never perish*.

Wang pondered these words, then looked around him. Had Secretary Wu wanted to flood this place to wipe away the memory of a shameful incident—shameful because the village Party Secretary was also the Snake Valley traitor? That would explain Wu's passion for the fish-farm project, and the neglect into which the memorial had been allowed to fall. But was it the truth?

''I'll probably never know,'' Wang said to himself. ''And if I don't know, I shouldn't drag the name of a good public servant into the dust.'' This thought reminded him of the Secretary's ideogram—''see through red dust'': maybe Wu had genuinely come to believe places like this didn't matter any longer. Everyone seemed to be thinking that way nowadays.

"They're wrong!" he said out loud, his voice petulant as a child's. "People are forgetting how bad the old China was. How harsh, how backward, how unjust. They mustn't!"

He crossed to the stone bench and sat down. The stream was babbling, as always: apart from that, Snake Valley was silent, as if in respect for the dead.

For all the dead.

Wang began reading the names on the plinth, but only got halfway before he broke off, shaking his head. This memorial told half a story, not a full one. There should be other names on it, too, if it were truly to commemorate the sufferings of his home village in this turbulent century. The Xu family, for example.

"Landlords!" an inner voice objected.

Victims, he replied to it.

He pondered this for a while, then got up, gathered a stick and traced three characters in the lichen on the plinth.

Xu Yi Feng.

As he did so, he heard the voice object, even louder.

"Sorry, father," he said defiantly. And he added another name, the scapegoat Shen Zirong.

Then he looked at his watch. Time to head home. To the city.

GLOSSARY & LIST OF HISTORICAL FIGURES

Ai, Aiya!	Exclamation of surprise or disappointment
Cadre	Senior Party official
County	Administrative sub-unit of state
Cultural Revolution	Period of turmoil instigated by Mao Zedong. At its worst 1967–1973, but did not subside totally until 1976
Fengshui	Ancient Chinese art of geomancy
Ganbei!	Cheers!
Guomindang	Nationalists, opponents of Communists in 1940s Civil War
Heilongjiang	"Black Dragon River," China's northernmost province
Jiaozi	Meat-filled dumplings popular in north China
Jinan	State capital of Shandong province
Kang Sheng	Corrupt, Shandong-born Party leader (d. 1975)

Land Reform	Movement in 1950s that classified country-dwellers by their status in pre–Revolutionary China and distributed land to them (in inverse proportion to that status)
Lei Feng	Ideal Maoist soldier, "goody-goody"
Li	Unit of length, about a kilometre
Liberation	1949 (End of 1940s Civil War, in victory for Chairman Mao)
Maotai	Clear, strong alcoholic spirit
PSB	Public Security Bureau (i/c Police)
Qi	Life-force in traditional Chinese medicine
Qigong	Traditional art of meditation / keep-fit
Qing	Last imperial dynasty (1644–1911)
Qingdao	Seaside resort in Shandong province
Red Guards	Fanatical supporters of Cultural Revolution
Rightist	Label for political opponent in Mao era
Shandong	Rural central/northern province. Wang's birthplace
Sichuan	Remote western province
Wushu	Martial arts
Xiangqi	Chinese chess
Yan'an	Communist base during Civil War
Yuan	Basic unit of Chinese currency